Justin Ladd

ABILENE

THE
SHARPSHOOTER

G.K.HALL &CO.
Boston, Massachusetts
1989

2-89   Publ 1500

Copyright © 1988 by Book Creations, Inc.
Cover artwork copyright © 1988 Gordon Crabb.

Published in Large Print by arrangement with
Pocket Books.

G.K. Hall Large Print Book Series.

Set in 16 pt Plantin.

Library of Congress Cataloging in Publication Data

Ladd, Justin.
  The sharpshooter / Justin Ladd.
      p.   cm.—(G.K. Hall large print book series) (Nightingale
series)
   ISBN 0-8161-4719-1 (lg. print)
   1. Large type books.   I. Title.
[PS3562.A259S58 1989]
813'.54—dc19   88-25960

"You come back to see us, Marshal," the pretty redheaded young woman in a waitress's apron said cheerfully as Luke Travis stepped out the door of the Sunrise Café.

"I will, Agnes," the lawman called over his shoulder with a grin. "You can count on that."

In two easy strides Travis crossed the wide boardwalk and stood at its edge as he scanned Texas Street. The brightly colored signs on the two- and three-story frame and clapboard buildings that lined the broad street sparkled in the morning sun. Travis had just finished an excellent breakfast of ham and hotcakes, washed down with plenty of strong coffee, and he now paused to relish the crisp spring air as he surveyed his town.

Lounging casually against one of the posts supporting the awning over the boardwalk, Travis appeared deceptively lazy; his tall, well-muscled frame was relaxed. Dressed in denim work clothes and calf-high riding boots, he looked like any cowpuncher; only the badge pinned to his tan vest spoke of his occupation. Under his hat, which was tipped down to shade the sun from his lean face, his eyes were alert and watchful. He was not expecting trouble, but he was ready if it came.

Luke Travis had not been marshal of Abilene for long, but in that short time he had won the respect and trust of its citizens. Years before, he had served as the marshal of Wichita for quite some time and had earned his reputation as a tough, honest lawman who was widely known in Kansas. But it was in Wichita that tragedy struck—a bullet meant for Travis wounded his beloved wife, Sarah, and took them both back east. After years of wasting away despite the efforts of the finest physicians, his brave, joyful Sarah died, leaving Travis alone and empty to make the painful journey back from his loss. He had hung up his walnut-handled Peacemaker in its well-worn leather gun belt, intending never to strap it on again. But events had changed his mind and brought him to this fine spring morning, to the bustling town he now proudly called home.

Travis pushed his tan, flat-crowned hat back on his head, revealing the silver streaks that shot through his sandy hair at the temples. Even at this time of the morning, Abilene's main thoroughfare was alive with activity. Teamsters cracked their whips, and heavy draft horses pulled freight wagons loaded with canvas-covered, tied-down goods. Farmers drove buckboards up to the stores to pick up supplies. Several buggies rolled here and there carrying early-rising businessmen, and as always there were men on horseback—cowboys and drifters and probably even a few desperadoes, though they would keep a low profile while they were in Abilene. Word had gotten around that Luke Travis was in charge now.

As the breeze shifted slightly, Travis caught a hint of the pungent aroma of the Great Western Cattle Company's stockyards on the eastern edge of town. The marshal smiled slightly. That odor was at the core of Abilene's existence—the great herds of long-horns moving up the trails from Texas to meet the tracks and terminals of the new Kansas Pacific Railroad that stretched across the country linking towns like Abilene to

the great markets. Wealth and prosperity—
and more than a little trouble—had come
right along with this rapid growth in the
Kansas plains.

Travis ran a thumb over his drooping
brown mustache and nodded a greeting to a
passing townsman. He looked beyond the
man, his gaze following Texas Street to the
east, and then his eyes narrowed.

Coming down the street, just passing the
courthouse, was a small wagon driven by a
stranger. In Abilene, such a sight was not
unusual, but Travis had the instincts of a
good lawman, and he now sensed impending trouble.

Travis watched the wagon as its driver
pulled the two-horse team to a stop just
before the intersection with Buckeye Street,
over two blocks away. Travis had sharp eyes,
but at this distance he could make out little
about the man other than his gray suit and
the black derby perched on his head. As
Travis watched, the driver hopped down
and tied his team to the hitch rail. He went
to the back of the wagon, opened a box
sitting there, and took out a handful of pa-
pers.

Straightening, Travis saw the man start
up the boardwalk, heading toward him. The

stranger took out a small hammer that had been tucked behind his belt and, fishing out tacks from his pocket, began posting the sheets on the walls of the buildings and the boardwalk posts.

The man moved rather quickly, despite a pronounced limp. He worked his way up the street, crossed Spruce Street, and nailed up several of his posters on the wall of Karatofsky's Great Western Store.

With his rapid pace, the man had worked his way past the jail and was now directly opposite Travis. Even across the wide street, Travis could see clearly the gaudy colors and fancy lettering on the posters. As the man moved on, continuing with his work, Travis stepped out into the street.

As Travis waited for a moment to let several freight wagons pass, three men in range clothes staggered out of the Bull's Head Saloon a few doors away. From their loud voices and boisterous behavior, Travis guessed that they had probably been in the saloon all night, carousing and guzzling liquor—that being the favorite pastime of most cowboys passing through Abilene.

Travis shifted his attention away from the three young men, who would undoubtedly find a place to sleep off their binge. At the moment, he was more interested in what the posters had to say.

He stepped onto the boardwalk and studied one of them, attached to a nearby post. His forehead creased in a frown as he took in the brightly colored drawing of a huge striped tent surrounded by exotic-looking animals. There were lions and tigers and elephants, camels and giraffes and apes. In addition to the animals, beautiful girls in scanty costumes did tricks on horseback, a bald-headed man wore an animal skin and bent a metal bar in his hands, several clowns engaged in foolishness, and a pretty girl in buckskins fired two Colts toward a target. The big letters at the top of the poster proclaimed SEE PROFESSOR JERICHO JEFFRIES'S WORLD-RENOWNED TRAVELING CIRCUS AND EXTRAVAGANZA. Smaller letters at the bottom read: Thrills, Chills, Excitement and Fun for All Ages! Coming Soon to Your City!

Travis's frown turned to a look of amusement. The circus was coming to Abilene. That would provide some excitement for the town, all right. Most of the folks around Abilene had most likely never seen a circus.

The frown returned, however, as Travis began to remember stories he had heard about the disruptions such a traveling show could cause.

A loud bray of laughter snapped him out of his thoughts, and he looked up the block to see that the three drunken cowboys had also crossed the street and had paused to study one of the advertisements. Not content to leave it on the wall where the stranger had tacked it, they had ripped the poster down and were passing it from hand to hand, making coarse comments about the trick riders in spangled costumes.

One of the cowboys, a tall, wide-shouldered, sandy-haired young man with rough-hewn features, jabbed a blunt finger at the poster and asked, "How'd you like to go bareback ridin' with this one, boys?"

"Damn right, Cahoon," one of his companions replied. "As long as it was her back that was bare!"

The crude witticism provoked another howl of laughter from the third man. The one called Cahoon started to say something else but stopped when he noticed the man putting up the posters.

"Look at that feller," Cahoon said, slapping one of his companions on the shoulder and pointing to the stranger. "Right spry for a cripple, ain't he?"

If the man heard the harsh words, he gave no sign of it. He continued with his work, ignoring the cowboys.

Travis started down the block toward the three drunken men. It was time for them to move along. Also, he wanted to have a word with the stranger.

Cahoon crumpled the poster in his hand and tossed it into the street. Then with a mischievous leer on his face, he swung around and started after the stranger, his two cohorts following right behind.

"Hey, mister!" Cahoon called to the man. "Wait up a minute!"

The stranger stopped and turned toward the cowboys, an expression of polite interest on his handsome, clean-shaven face. He was a fairly young man, in his early thirties perhaps, with dark curly hair under the derby. He nodded and said, "Good morning, gents. What can I do for you?"

Cahoon pointed at the poster the man had just nailed up. "We was just lookin' at your signs about the circus," he said.

"Yeah," one of the other cowboys chimed in. "The way you scamper along, we was wonderin' if you're one of the trained monkeys."

The slight smile remained on the stranger's face, but his eyes blazed with anger. Travis, still several yards away down the boardwalk, stopped abruptly, wanting to hear the man's response and see how he handled himself.

Controlling his anger and smiling even more broadly, the stranger replied, "No, sir, those apes can do tricks that would put my efforts to shame. Why, all of our animals are so talented and well trained that you won't believe your eyes when you see them. You boys *will* be attending the circus, won't you?"

"I don't rightly know," Cahoon said, put off guard by the stranger's friendly attitude.

"Well, you should. I promise you, you've never seen anything like it before. Wild animals, trick riders, acrobats—you name it, and Professor Jericho Jeffries has got it." He slapped the thigh of his bad leg and grinned. "Used to be an acrobat myself, I did, until I got this bum leg. Tell you what, fellas." Still smiling, he reached inside his coat and pulled out several slips of paper. "I'll give you these complimentary passes if you'll tell all your friends about the circus. You just tell them Gil Palmer said they should come and have the time of their lives."

Cahoon stared at the passes in the man's extended hand for a moment, and then his mouth twisted in a sneer. He slapped the free tickets aside. "You think you can brush us off like that, mister?" he said roughly. "Hell, if we're botherin' you, just say so."

Waiting in the doorway of a store, Travis decided it was time to put a stop to this. Several bystanders were pausing to watch, and soon a crowd would gather.

But as Travis silently took a step forward, his eyes locked with Gil Palmer's, and he saw the man's head shake no, almost imperceptibly, as if to motion him away. Travis halted. There was some quality about the man that made Travis hesitate to interfere against his wishes. Somehow, the stranger gave the impression that he had things under control.

When Palmer made no reply to Cahoon's gibe, one of the other cowboys sprang forward. "We don't want to bother you, mister," he said with a cackle. "We're helpful fellers, ain't we?" He snatched the handful of posters away from Palmer. "Hell, we can't let a poor cripple work so hard. Come on, boys, we'll put these posters up!"

Palmer's tight control finally began to slip away. He reached out and tried to grasp the sheaf of advertisements. "Give me those," he said sharply.

The cowboy put a hand against Palmer's chest and shoved. "I told you we'd help," he growled. He tossed the posters toward the third man, who made no effort to catch them. They fell to the boardwalk, scattering.

Seeing that the breeze threatened to blow several of the posters away, Palmer lunged toward them, reaching down to recover them. But as he did so, Cahoon thrust out a booted foot, tripping him, and Palmer pitched forward. He caught himself before sprawling on the boardwalk, however, quickly recovering his balance. Anger was plain on his face as he spun around, the posters forgotten now.

Cahoon's open palm thumped against Palmer's shoulder, staggering the smaller man. "You want to fight?" he laughed.

Palmer drew back his arm and hurled a fist at the cowboy, catching him on the jaw. Calhoon's head snapped around. Palmer had moved faster than anyone would have expected, and his punch obviously packed some power. Cahoon stepped backward, involuntarily.

Taking advantage of the stunned surprise

that momentarily held Cahoon's friends motionless, Palmer turned toward them. He grabbed the arm of one of the men and pivoted, jerking the man against his hip and then bending. The cowboy howled in protest as he suddenly found himself flying through the air. When he slammed against the planks of the boardwalk, the air was knocked from his lungs.

The third man had recovered enough to realize that Palmer was a bigger threat than he appeared. The cowboy threw himself at the stranger, gripping him in a bear hug.

Palmer countered by going limp and falling forward, causing the cowboy to lose his balance. Both men fell. Palmer twisted and somehow landed on top. He drove a knee into his attacker's belly, rolled to the side, slapped a palm against the boardwalk to catch himself, and bounded back onto his feet.

Watching the fight, Travis could easily believe that Palmer had been an acrobat. Despite his bad leg, the stranger was remarkably agile.

The odds were simply too much, though. By the time Palmer regained his feet, Cahoon had recovered from the first punch and was waiting. The cowboy's knobby fist lashed out, cracking into Palmer's jaw. Palmer was knocked backward, only to be caught by the second man, who had just gotten back onto his feet. The man grabbed Palmer's arms from behind and launched a kick that thudded into the former acrobat's injured leg. Palmer's face contorted in agony.

"Hold the bastard!" Cahoon yelled as he stepped in, drawing back a fist to slam it into Palmer's stomach.

The blow never landed. Travis caught Cahoon's shoulder and thrust him to one side. "That's enough!" the lawman rasped. "Break it up!"

Cahoon's face was livid with fury. Not only had Palmer dared to hit him, but now someone else was butting in to interrupt his fun. Disregarding the newcomer's identity, Cahoon snarled a curse and dropped his hand to the big pistol on his hip. The burly cowboy was fast on the draw, but his gun had just cleared leather when the long barrel of Travis's Colt .44 cracked across his wrist. Cahoon yelped in pain as the pistol slipped from his numbed fingers.

"Take it easy, son," Travis warned as he stepped back slightly and pointed his gun at Cahoon's middle.

Cahoon was too enraged to be stopped by

Travis's words of caution. Disarmed, he leaped toward Travis and swung.

Travis moved smoothly to one side and let the wild punch slide by harmlessly. There was going to be no reasoning with Cahoon, he saw. But he did not want to shoot the young man, either.

Dropping his pistol back into its holster, Travis blocked Cahoon's next punch and threw one of his own. His fist smacked into Cahoon's solar plexus, and then before the cowboy could react, the marshal caught him with a powerful hook that sent him off the edge of the boardwalk and into the street. Dust flew as Cahoon landed heavily.

Travis whirled to face the other two cowboys. One of them was still holding Palmer, and the other was climbing shakily onto his feet. Both men now stared at Travis, painfully aware of the badge on his vest as well as the blinding speed of his draw.

Glancing at Cahoon's motionless form sprawled in the street, Travis turned to the other two men and said, "You boys want to move along peacefully, or do we continue this little dance?"

The one holding Palmer suddenly jerked his hands away and stepped back. "Hold on, Marshal," he said quickly. "We was just funnin'. We don't want no trouble."

Released from the man's grip, Palmer sagged against the railing at the edge of the boardwalk and took a deep breath.

The other cowboy joined his companion in backing away, his hands outstretched to show how harmless he was. "Honest, Marshal, we won't cause no more trouble," he declared.

Travis glanced toward the crowd of bystanders and grimaced. He never should have let this thing go so far. Palmer could have been seriously injured.

"You two stand still," he barked at the two cowboys. He stepped over to Palmer's side and asked the man, "Are you all right?"

Palmer straightened and brushed the dust off his gray suit coat. "I'm fine, Marshal," he said. "I appreciate the help." He bent to pick up his derby, which had been knocked off during the scuffle.

Travis nodded toward the two nervous punchers and asked Palmer, "You want to press charges against them and their friend?"

Palmer glanced at the cowboys and then at the watching townspeople. He smiled ruefully. "I don't think so, Marshal," he said in a low-pitched voice. "It's not good business for an outsider to come in and have some local boys thrown in jail."

"You'd be within your rights to file a complaint."

Palmer shook his head. "I think they've learned their lesson. Especially the one you decked."

Travis grunted. He was not as confident as Palmer that Cahoon and his friends had learned anything from this experience. "All right," he said. "Whatever you want." He jerked a thumb at where Cahoon was lying and spoke to the other two cowboys. "You two get your friend out of here. I don't want to see any of you around until you've had time to cool off. Understand?"

The two men bobbed their heads. "Yes, sir, Marshal," one of them said. "We surely do."

While Travis and Palmer watched, they stepped down from the boardwalk and hurried to Cahoon's recumbent form. Bending over, each one grasped him under an arm and lifted him to his feet. "Come on, Ned," one of the men told him urgently. "We got to get out of here."

Cahoon let out a moan and shook his head, but his friends turned him around and steered him across the street toward a trio of horses that were tied up in front of the Bull's Head. Cahoon was moving under his own power by the time they reached the animals, although he was staggering slightly and had to be helped to mount up. Once he was on the back of his horse, Cahoon took the lead. As the little group passed Travis and Palmer, Cahoon glowered at them.

Palmer watched them ride toward the western edge of town, then sighed and turned to Travis. "I'd say that fellow is not the type to forgive and forget."

"I expect you're right about that," Travis allowed. "I don't know the boy, but I've seen plenty like him. Maybe he'll head back to Texas instead of staying around to even the score."

Palmer grinned. "Well, I have other things to worry about." He gestured toward the scattered circus posters. "For one thing, I have a job to do."

"I was coming to talk to you about that." Travis began helping Palmer gather up the posters. "I think it would be a good idea if you got the owners' permission before you put up these posters on buildings all over town."

"Of course, Marshal. I'll go back down

the street and make sure no one objects to the ones I've already put up."

Travis grinned at him. "Good idea. But that can wait. Come have a cup of coffee with me first." The lawman extended his hand. "I'm Luke Travis."

"Gil Palmer." The former acrobat returned the handshake. His grip was as firm as Travis had expected it to be. "I'm glad to meet you, Marshal."

"Same here." Travis started across the street toward the Sunrise Café. "Now, tell me all about this circus you've got coming to town."

Palmer grinned. "Marshal, I can promise you, Abilene has never seen anything like it."

Travis nodded. That was what he was afraid of.

"Professor Jeffries's show is one of the best traveling circuses in the country today," Gil Palmer declared as he and Travis crossed the street. "We've played in all the major cities in the East and performed before some of the crowned heads of Europe. Our attractions are truly world famous, Marshal."

Travis grinned. "And you wouldn't tell me any different, would you?"

Palmer laughed as he stepped lightly up

18

onto the boardwalk. "My job is to promote the circus, Mr. Travis. I like to think that I'm good at it."

Travis opened the door and stepped back to let Palmer precede him into the café. The inviting aroma of fresh brewed coffee and baking bread greeted them as they walked into the cheerful, clean dining room. Several tables covered with bright red-checked cloths and set for four were spaced around the room, and a long counter stood a few feet from the right wall. Agnes Hirsch, the young redheaded waitress, was standing just inside the door. "I saw the fight, Marshal," she said excitedly. "I thought for a second that cowboy was going to shoot you!"

"I did, too, Agnes," Travis replied dryly. "That's why I made sure that he didn't." He took off his hat and dropped it on one of the tables as he pulled out a chair and sat down. "How about bringing us a couple cups of coffee?"

Agnes nodded and went behind the counter to pour the coffee. There were several other customers in the establishment, all of whom had evidently watched the fracas through the windows, for they called out words of congratulations to Travis. The marshal, wishing so much would not be made of a simple fight, nodded in acknowl-edgment.

Eagerly, Agnes brought the two steaming cups of coffee to the table where Travis and Palmer were seated.

"Is there anything else I can get you, Marshal?" Agnes asked as she placed the coffee on the table.

Travis shook his head. "Not for me. How about you, Mr. Palmer? Some breakfast?"

"Thanks, but I already ate on the trail," Palmer replied, gazing at Agnes in frank appreciation. Her pale-skinned, green-eyed loveliness was just blossoming into a mature beauty. He smiled warmly and then contin-ued. "I like to make an early start."

Blushing, Agnes smiled and went back to the counter. Palmer watched her go.

"Pretty girl," he said with a nod.

"And a nice one," Travis said protec-tively. He did not want Palmer, who was no doubt used to a different type of woman, to get any wrong ideas about Agnes. She had arrived in Abilene at the same time as Travis, traveling with her younger brother and over a dozen other orphans who were now living in a makeshift orphanage at the Calvary Methodist Church. The youngsters were un-der the combined care of the Reverend Judah

Fisher, the pastor of the church, and Sister Laurel, the Dominican nun who had brought them to Abilene.

Palmer smiled and sipped the hot coffee. "Now, Marshal, what else would you like to know about the circus?"

"For one thing, when will it be here?"

"The wagons will roll in tomorrow morning, and as usual we'll be putting on a gala parade to celebrate the circus's arrival. If, of course, that's all right with you, Marshal. We try to abide by all local laws and ordinances in the towns we visit."

Travis frowned slightly. "A parade, eh? That ought to get the town all excited."

"We like to give the folks a good sample of what they'll be seeing if they purchase a ticket," Palmer said with a smile.

"All right," Travis said after considering for a moment. "I don't want to deny the town a chance for some excitement. Our people are good, hard-working citizens who deserve some entertainment whenever they can get it."

"Precisely. That's our mission in life, Marshal, to bring joy and excitement to the common man."

Palmer's voice was sincere, Travis decided. He was curious about Palmer's former occupation, however, and although the marshal did not want to call up any bad memories for the man, he decided to indulge his curiosity a bit. "You said you used to be an acrobat," he commented, leaving it up to Palmer whether or not to reply.

"An aerialist, actually," Palmer said. "I worked on the trapeze and the high wire." He paused. "Have you ever been to a circus, Marshal?"

Travis shook his head. "I lived back East for a while, though, and saw plenty of advertising posters for them, like the ones you've got there." He gestured at the stack of sheets that Palmer had placed on the table.

"Then you've seen pictures of the trapeze artists. That's what I did, and I don't mind saying, I was damned good at it." For the first time, the eager salesman's confidence flagged. His bright eyes clouded in a faraway look. "I was one of the best, Marshal . . . until the accident."

Travis said nothing.

"I was quite a daring young man," Palmer finally said with a grin. "Always eager to try some new stunt that hadn't been attempted before. I learned my craft from some of the best aerialists in Europe, and I suppose I wanted to top them. One night I tried one too many somersaults in midair and came up short of my catcher." He shrugged. "It was a long way to the ground. I was mighty lucky just to break my leg in three places—luckier still that it healed up enough for me to get around."

"You were with this Jeffries's circus then?" Travis asked.

Palmer nodded. "I've been with Jericho for a long time. When I was able to walk again, he offered me the job I've got now. I travel a day or two ahead of the circus and put up posters, trying to drum up plenty of interest in the show. It's not a bad life."

Travis shook his head and said, "I would have thought that after what happened, you wouldn't want to be around the circus."

"Ah, but there's where you're wrong, Marshal," Palmer said. "You can't understand, because the circus isn't in your blood. Once you've traveled with a show, smelled the sawdust, heard the delighted roar of the crowd . . . Well, it's just not something you can leave behind."

Travis nodded. Although he did not understand circus life and its appeal, he knew from his own experience how a man's chosen profession seemed to follow him around, tugging on him.

"Of course, everything would have been different if I'd been using a net," Palmer went on. "I'd probably still be working on the trapeze."

"A net?"

Palmer nodded. "It's a recent innovation. A large net is stretched out underneath the performers, high enough off the ground to catch them and prevent serious injuries should they fall. Most aerialists wouldn't use them when they were first introduced, but they're becoming more popular now." He smiled wryly. "I suppose we've all seen too many accidents." Pain flashed across his face, but Travis could tell that it was emotional, not physical.

"I suppose Jeffries uses a net in his shows now," the marshal said.

"He does, but my accident wasn't the cause. Jericho put the decision to the rest of the troupe after I fell, and they decided to continue without a net." There was a trace of bitterness in his voice as he went on. "I suppose they thought using a net cast some sort of doubt on their courage and honor. It took a tragedy a few months ago to change their minds."

"One of the other acrobats fell?"

"Professor Jeffries's wife, Mary. She was broken like a child's doll and didn't live for an hour after she fell." Palmer clenched his hands. "I warned her. I warned all of them. But they said they were paid to take chances."

Palmer stared down at the tablecloth for a long moment.

Travis rubbed his jaw. He had done the very thing he had intended not to do: stir up bad memories for the other man. Travis liked Gil Palmer and admired the man's courage and determination.

The bell on the café door jingled, breaking the silence that had fallen between the two men. Travis glanced up to his right and recognized the dark-haired young man dressed in black who strode through the door and then paused to scan the room.

Spotting Travis and Palmer, the man began to thread his way among the tables, heading toward them. Beneath his black hat his ruggedly handsome features broke into an easy grin as he approached. Arriving at the table, he reversed one of the vacant chairs, straddled it, and cuffed his hat back, revealing a faint, jagged scar that ran down his right cheek. "'Morning, Marshal," he said. "I hear there was some trouble."

Travis shrugged. "Some cowboys had too much to drink and picked a fight with Mr. Palmer here. Mr. Palmer, this is my deputy, Cody Fisher."

Palmer extended his hand. "Glad to meet you," Cody said as he shook it. His eye fell on the stack of posters, and he continued excitedly. "Say, you're the fellow who's been putting up those handbills about the circus! I saw one across the street."

"Yes, indeed," Palmer said. "It's true, Deputy. Professor Jericho Jeffries's Traveling Circus and Extravaganza is coming to Abilene."

Travis noticed that the volume of Palmer's voice rose as he spoke. Several heads in the café turned as the other customers listened to him. Travis had a hunch as to what was about to happen.

"I've never been to a circus before," Cody said. "Does the show have all the stuff that's in that picture on the handbill?"

"Does it? Why, young man, it has those attractions and much, much more!" Palmer glanced at Travis. "With your permission, Marshal . . . ?"

26

Travis shrugged his shoulders. A smile tugged at the corners of his broad mouth.

Palmer stood up, raising his arms and saying, "Ladies and gentlemen, your attention, please!" He picked up one of the posters and turned so that all of the other customers could see it.

"As you're no doubt aware, ladies and gentlemen," Palmer continued, "the circus is coming to Abilene. Yes, that's right, the circus! Tomorrow morning, a spectacular parade right down Texas Street will herald the arrival in your fair city of Professor Jericho Jeffries's Traveling Circus and Extravaganza. Known the world over, this troupe of performers will thrill and delight and astound you!" He picked up several more of the posters and handed them to a man at a nearby table. "Pass those around, would you, my good man, and be sure to keep one for yourself. Now, ladies and gentlemen, as you'll see from these complimentary handbills, Professor Jeffries's circus features only the most exciting, the most daring acts to be found anywhere. Why, here in your very own hometown, you can see legendary performers who have dazzled the princes and princesses of Europe, not to mention the cream of Eastern society in our own country! Right here in Abilene, folks, under the big top!"

There was a buzz of excited conversation in the room as Palmer paused in his speech. The man glanced at Travis, and Travis saw a sparkle of laughter in his eyes. He was a born pitchman, Travis thought, able to make folks believe just about anything he wanted them to.

Palmer continued his spiel for several minutes, keeping his audience enthralled, and when he finally ran out of words, he thanked the people in the café for their attention. Turning back to the table where Travis and Cody were seated, he gathered up the rest of his posters and drank what was left of his coffee, which had grown cold. "I'll be seeing you, Marshal. It was nice talking to you, but I've got to get back to work." He started to reach into his pocket to pull out some coins to pay for the coffee.

Travis held up a hand to stop him. "Coffee's on me," he said. "I should have stepped in earlier and stopped Cahoon and his friends from jumping you."

Palmer shook his head, and for the first time, Travis thought he saw a trace of resentment in the man's eyes. "Like I said, Marshal, I appreciated the help, but I could have handled those roughnecks. You live around a circus for a while, you learn how to take care of yourself."

"I suppose so, but around here, that sort of thing is my job."

Palmer smiled. "I understand. Thanks again, Marshal, for the coffee . . . and for everything else."

"Just remember to get permission before you tack up any more of those things."

Palmer promised to do that. He started toward the door, carrying his handbills and pausing to slap several of the customers on the back and talk to them individually.

"Friendly fellow," Cody said when the door had closed behind Palmer.

"That he is," Travis agreed.

Cody leaned forward. "What do you think about this circus coming to town, Marshal? I expect it'll be the most excitement Abilene's seen in a long time."

Excitement. Was that what Cody Fisher was all about? Travis asked himself as he looked at his young deputy. He was educated, had tried his hand at several trades, and had been on the run, not from the law but from the next young tough who could outshoot him. He had come to Abilene to avenge a murder and had unexpectedly found a home. In all respects he had been an excellent deputy, but Travis knew that there was an impulsive streak in Cody that might flare up at the wrong moment.

"Could be. I just hope it doesn't make a lot of extra work for you and me, Cody."

Cody frowned and started to ask a question, but before he could he was interrupted by the arrival of Agnes Hirsch, who stood next to the table and gazed down at him with adoring eyes. "Can I get you something, Cody?" she asked. "Some coffee or some breakfast?"

Cody smiled up at her. "I could sure use some scrambled eggs and hotcakes, maybe some bacon with it. And plenty of coffee."

"Sure, Cody. I'll tell the cook."

When Agnes had left the table, Cody grinned somewhat sheepishly at Travis. "The gal appears to like me," he said in a low voice.

"Is that so?" Travis grunted. Agnes's feelings for Cody were no secret to anyone with eyes.

"You were talking about the circus causing trouble," Cody prompted.

Travis nodded. "I've heard quite a bit about those shows," he said. "All kinds of con artists tend to follow them around, trying to make money any way they can off the people who attend the performances. Not to mention the sideshows themselves. Most of the time they're crooked. There are plenty of ways to relieve unsuspecting folks of their cash."

"Well, we'll keep an eye on 'em," Cody said confidently. "There won't be any of that around here. Anyway, maybe this Jericho fellow operates differently."

"Let's hope so."

A few minutes later Agnes arrived at the table with a big plate of food for Cody and a mug of steaming coffee. As she put the plate in front of him, Cody said, "Maybe you should be in that circus, Agnes. It takes a lot of talent to do what you do. And you're as pretty as any of those circus gals."

"Do you really think so, Cody?" She flushed with pleasure at the compliment.

"Wouldn't have said it if I didn't." Cody smiled gallantly at her, sending her back to the counter with a big grin on her face. "I really think you're worrying for nothing, Marshal," Cody went on. He snapped his fingers. "Say, I think I've heard of this Professor Jericho before. He's got some pretty young gal in his show who's a sharp-shooter."

Travis remembered the drawing on the poster of the girl in buckskins shooting at a target. "Could be you're right," he said. *Trust Cody to have heard about a pretty woman,* he thought.

"Yep, I'm sure I am." Cody's eyes narrowed. "Think she could outshoot me, Marshal?"

Travis chuckled dryly. "Maybe I can find out for you. I plan to visit this Jericho Jeffries just as soon as the circus arrives in town."

"Going to lay down the law to him, eh?"

"I just want to make sure he and his people understand that they're not to cause trouble while they're here," Travis replied quietly.

"Well, in that case I'd better go along, since it's an official visit and all. Maybe I can talk to the lady sharpshooter myself."

Travis was not surprised that Cody was inviting himself along. He had expected the deputy to do just that. And to tell the truth, he would not mind Cody's presence. *It never hurts to have a good man at your side,* Travis thought.

II

Gil Palmer had been gone from the café for several minutes and Travis and Cody were finishing their coffee when they heard a commotion outside. The clamor of church bells ringing loudly made Cody drop his cup. Shouts from the street mingled with the ringing of the bells, but the lawmen were able to make out one word clearly: *"Fire!"*

Travis and Cody reacted more quickly than the others in the café and, leaping to their feet, were the first ones to reach the door. As they rushed outside, they saw a large crowd racing up the street.

Cody caught Travis's arm and pointed. "Look there, Marshal!"

Travis saw the thick black smoke rising above the buildings a few blocks north, on the other side of the railroad tracks. "Come on!" he yelled as he started running toward the blaze. He and Cody soon joined the press of townspeople heading for the scene of the fire. They pushed their way through the crowd, the clamor of bells still ringing in their ears.

As they ran across the Kansas Pacific tracks, Travis scanned the buildings ahead. He could not see flames yet, but as they approached, he saw smoke billowing from a warehouse on Fourth Street. It was the old abandoned Hanzlick Freight Company warehouse—a large, three-story brick building, nearly windowless and standing alone on its lot.

As Travis and Cody pounded up, one of the big, boarded-up doors suddenly collapsed, eaten away by the fire inside. Flames licked out of the opening, and the smoke billowing into the blue sky suddenly became thicker as more air was fed to the conflagration.

"What the hell?" Cody shouted.

Travis spun to face him. "Get a bucket brigade started," he ordered sharply. "It looks like the fire's only on the first floor. Maybe we can stop it from spreading upstairs or at least protect the other buildings."

Cody nodded and began grabbing bystanders and issuing orders. Some men ran to fetch buckets, while others began forming a line that would stretch all the way back to the town well.

Travis looked around, trying to find

someone who might know what had happened here, and he spotted a familiar figure standing in a knot of men several yards away. Gil Palmer and some of the townspeople were surrounding a tall, gangly youth, who was covered with soot and ashes. Coughs racked the boy's slender frame, and one of the bystanders pounded him on the back.

As Travis hurried over, Palmer glanced around and saw the lawman coming. "Here's the marshal," he said. The smoke-grimed youth staggered, and Palmer quickly grasped his arm to keep him from falling.

"What happened?" Travis asked curtly.

"I was putting up some of my handbills down the street when I saw the smoke, Marshal. I got over here as fast as I could." He nodded to the boy. "This young fellow was trying to break some boards out of one of the windows in the warehouse so he could climb out. I gave him a hand."

"Saved his life, that's what he did," one of the townsmen spoke up. "Hector'd'a smothered for sure in there if this feller hadn't pulled him out."

Travis looked at the teenager. "Are you all right, son?"

A fresh spasm of coughing shook Hector.

When it was over, he gasped, "I . . . I'm all right. But you've gotta help Johnny!"

Travis caught the boy's other arm. "There's somebody else in there?" he asked urgently.

Hector nodded shakily. "He . . . he was on the other side of the fire. I c-couldn't get to him. Oh, God, Marshal, you've gotta get him out of there!"

Travis exchanged a grim glance with a couple of the men standing nearby. "You men go around back of the warehouse and see if the other boy got out that way," he ordered. They nodded and broke into a run, heading down the alley beside the blazing building.

Close by, Cody had the bucket brigade organized. Standing at the head of the line, he looked back toward the center of town to see the first of the water-filled buckets being passed toward him. It seemed like a futile effort to him, but they had to try to contain the fire.

Travis looked at Cody and the bucket brigade, saw that everything possible was being done to fight the fire, and glanced again at the building. The smoke coming from it was even thicker and blacker now. Turning back to Hector, who was still being held up by Gil Palmer, he asked, "What the devil were you boys doing in that place?"

Hector shook his head and coughed again. Before he could answer, another man pushed into the circle around the youth and said stridently, "I'll tell you what they were doing, Marshal. They were playing hooky from school, the little . . . little . . ." The newcomer was sputtering so with rage that he had to give up before finishing his statement.

Travis recognized the undersized body and sour expression belonging to Thurman Simpson, the local schoolmaster. He had met Simpson a couple of times and had not been very impressed. Simpson had struck him as pompous and overbearing, and he had a reputation as a strict disciplinarian in the schoolhouse.

In a gentler tone, Travis asked, "What about it, son? Were you playing hooky? More importantly, were there just the two of you in there?"

Hector nodded. "Yeah, Marshal. It was just me and Johnny." The boy cast a glance of thinly veiled hatred toward the schoolmaster. "It was such a nice day, we didn't feel like . . . like bein' yelled at all day. So we just didn't go. Johnny, he said he knew a way to sneak into the warehouse, so we took a lantern and did that instead. We . . . we found some old cigars in there and decided to smoke 'em—" His voice broke as he went on. "I—I knocked the lantern over. . . . There was nothing I could do, the fire spread so fast."

Thurman Simpson crossed his arms smugly. "And you see what your little adventure got you?" he said sarcastically. "You're in trouble, and your friend has probably suffered an agonizing death by fire."

"That's enough of that," Travis snapped. "You can have your say later, Simpson."

The schoolmaster glared at him but kept quiet.

The men Travis had sent to check the rear of the building came running back with their report, the bad news written clearly on their faces. "There's no way out through the back," one of them said. "There's a door, but it's bolted on both sides. And nobody's messed with either of the windows."

"I could hear the flames crackling right on the other side of the door, Marshal," the other man added. "The fire's spread back there, and it'd be sure death to try to go in that way."

"Upstairs," Hector suddenly said. "I . . . I think maybe I heard Johnny running up the stairs."

Travis looked at the building. It was impossible to tell for sure, but he did not think the flames had reached the second floor of the warehouse yet. But even if they had not, they would within a matter of minutes.

"If the boy's up there, he has to be gotten out," Travis said. "And there's no way up there except through the fire."

He took off his hat and began unbuckling the shell belt and holster around his hips.

Gil Palmer left Hector's side and caught Travis's arm. "What do you think you're doing?" he demanded.

"My job," Travis answered flatly. He jerked his arm free from Palmer's grip, pulled a bandanna from his pocket and began tying it around his face, ignoring the protests that came from the bystanders.

"You can't go in there," Palmer insisted.

"There's no outside staircase," Travis pointed out impatiently. "How else can I get up there?" Without waiting for an answer, he ran over to the head of the bucket brigade.

Travis pulled a full bucket out of the hands of his startled deputy and dumped the contents over his head. Then he thrust the pail back at Cody and grated, "You're in charge now."

"What? . . . Hey, Marshal!"

Cody's cry was too late. Travis had ducked his head, lunged forward, and disappeared through the flame-choked opening.

Cody started to go after him, but some instinct held him back. Travis had put him in charge and had clearly expected him to stay outside and keep the bucket brigade going.

Torn by his emotions, Cody reached out to take the bucket of water from the next man in the line. He cursed as he flung the water through the door onto the flames.

Gil Palmer saw Travis vanish into the blaze, and he chewed his lip for a moment in frustration. He did not want to stand by idly while Luke Travis risked his life. But he knew that going inside through the flames would just add to Travis's burden.

Palmer glanced up. Something struck him about the architecture of the burning building. There were gargoyles at each corner of the roof, ugly squatting figures that might prove to be the answer.

Palmer looked around as the idea took hold, and he spotted a horse tied at the rail in front of one of the other buildings. His limp not slowing him, he rushed over to the animal. It shied away from him at first, but he patted its flank and spoke to it in a soothing voice that somehow penetrated the uproar in the street. When the horse had calmed down, Palmer took the coiled lariat that hung over the saddle horn.

A moment later, Cody felt a tug at his arm. He glanced over to see Palmer holding the rope. "Have you ever roped any cattle?" the man from the circus asked him urgently.

Cody stared at him, wondering if the fellow had gone crazy. "Sure, I've thrown a loop over plenty of steers," he said.

Palmer thrust the coiled rope at him. "Good! See if you can rope one of those gargoyles."

Cody looked up, narrowing his eyes. Suddenly he realized what Palmer had in mind. Far from crazy, Palmer had hit on just the thing they needed.

Assigning a man to replace him at the end of the line, Cody took the rope from Palmer. He shook out a loop and began twirling it slowly, gradually getting the rope to move faster and faster. When he was ready, he suddenly lashed out with his arm, snapping his wrist as he cast the loop up toward the top of the warehouse.

The rope fell short, striking the side of the building a good eight feet below the top.

Cody's mouth tightened as he hurriedly pulled the lariat back in and gathered the loop again. He tried once more, putting more strength into his throw this time. The crowd had noticed what he was trying to do, and the bystanders groaned as the second toss also missed.

His face grim, Cody prepared for another try. Although it had probably been only a minute since Travis had gone into the building, it already seemed like hours. Heat from the blaze blasted against Cody's face as he flung the loop one more time.

The throw was perfect, the loop widening out as it sailed through the air and then settling gently over the masonry figure at the corner of the building. With an exultant cry, Cody jerked it taut and then leaned on the line, testing it for strength and stability.

Palmer reached out and put his hand on the rope. "I'll climb it," he declared.

Cody shook his head. "Thanks, Mr. Palmer, but it's my job."

"Maybe so, but I've had years of experience at things like this, Deputy." Palmer grinned. "I used to make my living climbing up on things, remember?"

"What about your bad leg?" Cody asked.

"A climb like this requires a great deal of strength in the arms. The legs are used primarily for balance. And mine will do just fine for that."

Cody had to make a decision. This discussion was wasting time. Abruptly, he nodded and released the rope. "Good luck," he said sincerely.

Palmer grinned and, adjusting his poster-hanging hammer behind his belt, took hold of the rope with both hands. He leaned back slightly as he lifted a leg and placed his foot against the side of the building. Then, letting his arms take the weight of his body, he began walking up the wall of the warehouse.

He was vaguely aware of the excited buzz from the crowd as he started his ascent. It was reminiscent of all the times he had performed under the big top, and for a moment, things blurred for Palmer. He was back in the circus again, going through his act, thrilling and dazzling the audience with his daring, flying through the air alongside the beautiful Mary Jeffries—

A cloud of acrid smoke puffed into his face as he passed a boarded-up window on the second floor, bringing him back to a harsh, eye-stinging reality. The smoke was coming out through cracks around the boards. Palmer had already decided to try to get in through one of the single third-floor windows on this side of the building. That seemed to offer the best chance of avoiding the flames.

The climb itself was not difficult. Within moments, Palmer had reached the window that was his destination. It was boarded up like the others in the warehouse, but it had fewer planks nailed over it. Hanging onto the rope with his left hand, Palmer used his right to grasp his hammer. He did not glance down as he started prying one of the boards loose.

The nails were rusty and stubborn, but Palmer threw all the strength of his back and shoulders into the job, and the board came loose with a screech of nails. "Look out below!" he shouted as it dropped to the street. Several of the bystanders jumped back as the board fell.

It was joined a moment later by another one, then another. Palmer had a big enough opening to squeeze through now. The pane of glass beneath the boards seemed to be intact, but it took only a second to shatter it with the hammer. After knocking out the shards around the opening, Palmer eased his legs through it. Smoke poured out from the broken window as he slipped into the burning warehouse, taking the rope with him.

Down on the ground, Cody watched anxiously, peering upward at the window where Palmer had disappeared. The seconds stretched out and became minutes that seemed like eternities. A silence settled over the crowd. The bucket brigade continued its work, but everyone else was watching the window, just like Cody. The deputy took his attention off the warehouse long enough to glance at the crowd and spotted his brother Judah, the pastor of the Calvary Methodist Church. Judah's lips were moving soundlessly, and Cody realized that he was offering up a prayer.

Suddenly, a booted foot came crashing through the boards that remained on the window. When all the planks had been knocked loose, Gil Palmer appeared. It was hard to see through the smoke, but a cheer went up when the crowd saw that someone was with Palmer. Cody clenched a fist in triumph as he recognized the tall figure of Luke Travis. Cody saw that both Travis and Palmer were as grimy and soot-covered as the boy called Hector had been.

It was too early to celebrate, though. The men still had to get down from their precarious position. Besides, Travis was carrying something, and Cody's features became bleak as he realized that it was a body.

Palmer climbed out of the window, looped the rope around his wrist, and braced himself against the side of the building. Travis leaned out carefully, handing the body over to Palmer. The former acrobat sagged for a moment under the weight, but then he steadied himself. Carefully draping the body over his shoulder, Palmer started down.

Travis leaned out of the window, watching Palmer's descent and glancing up to see how the rope and the gargoyle were withstanding the weight.

There were men waiting to take the body from Palmer as he approached the ground. He handed the limp form down, then released the rope and dropped the last few feet, catching himself easily as he landed. Over the roar of the fire, he shouted, "Come on, Marshal!"

Travis reached out and grasped the rope,

then let himself swing away from the window. Moving less gracefully than Palmer, he came down the rope hand over hand, unable to master the art of walking down the wall as the man from the circus had. Still, he got the job done, and a minute later his booted feet touched solid ground. Coughing, Travis staggered away from the building.

Cody grasped his arm to help support him. Someone thrust a canteen into Travis's hands, and he drank thirstily from it to clear his throat.

Above, flames burst from the window where Travis and Palmer had made their escape.

"Are you all right, Marshal?" Cody asked anxiously.

Travis nodded. He splashed water from the canteen onto his hand and wiped away some of the soot from his face. "Tell the bucket brigade to give it up," he said. "There's nothing they can do to save the warehouse. Just make sure the fire doesn't spread to any of the other buildings."

Cody nodded and hurried away to pass along the marshal's orders.

Surrounded by the crowd, Palmer had lowered the body of the boy called Johnny to the ground. The press of people around them suddenly parted as a short, thick-bodied man with graying reddish hair and beard pushed some of the bystanders aside with one arm. With his other hand, he clutched the arm of an attractive brunette woman carrying a black bag.

"Make room here!" Orion McCarthy, one of Abilene's tavern keepers roared. "The doctor's coming through, dinna ye know!"

Dr. Aileen Bloom hurried through the path cleared by Orion and knelt beside the boy's body. She glanced up at Gil Palmer, who was breathing heavily and coughing. "Are you all right?" she asked.

Palmer nodded. "I'll be fine. Tend to the boy."

Aileen's trained fingers went to Johnny's throat, searching desperately for a pulse. She glanced up again a moment later and said, "He's alive!"

Another cheer went up from the crowd as the word spread. With the help of a couple of the men, Aileen got Johnny turned over. Placing her hands on his back, she began to push, in and out, in and out, trying to make the boy's lungs work on their own. After a few seconds, a great, shuddering spasm of coughing shook him. When that was finally over, his breathing settled into a more regular rhythm, although it was still hoarse and labored.

Aileen stood up and pushed back a lock of dark hair that had fallen into her face. "Get him on his feet and away from this smoke," she directed the men. Then she turned to look for Luke Travis. Spotting him, she hurried over.

He grinned tiredly at her as he met her anxious gaze. "Don't worry," he told her before she could ask. "I'll be fine as soon as I get the rest of that smoke out of me."

"Are you having trouble breathing?"

"A little soreness in my throat, but I figure that's normal enough after swallowing so much smoke. How's Palmer?"

"The other man who went into the warehouse? He says he's all right, but I want to take a look at him," Aileen declared.

With Travis at her side, she went to check on Palmer, who assured her that he was having no trouble breathing. Aileen looked from Travis to Palmer and shook her head. "You men are very lucky," she said. "You could have died from smoke inhalation, not to mention the danger from the fire itself."

Travis nodded. "I didn't have much choice as long as somebody was trapped in there." He looked at Palmer. "But you didn't have to go in after me."

Palmer grinned. "I just figured it was about time I put my training to good use."

"Well, you saved our lives," Travis said with a smile of respect. "I never would've gotten him out alone."

Nearby, Johnny was on his feet, leaning on his friend Hector. Both boys were a sight, their faces and clothes blackened with soot. Suddenly, Thurman Simpson's slender figure appeared in front of them.

"You young devils!" he lashed out. "I hope you're satisfied. You've burned down a building, nearly gotten Marshal Travis and that other man killed, and disrupted an entire day of schooling! Yes, I hope you're proud." The schoolmaster's voice shook with anger. "Now get on back to the school. There's a switch waiting for both of you!"

Drawn by Simpson's ranting, Travis walked over to the scene, accompanied by Aileen and Palmer. He heard Simpson's order to the boys and said, "I think it'd be better if these two fellows went home, Mr. Simpson. I'm sure they don't feel too well right now."

Still glaring at Hector and Johnny, Simpson shook his head and answered, "I don't care how they feel. They're going to class, where they should have been all along." He reached out and grasped Hector's ear, twisting brutally and yanking him away from his friend.

Travis's hand came down hard on Simpson's shoulder, and in a low voice, he grated, "I didn't risk my life for these boys just so that you could mistreat them, Simpson. You'd best think about what you're doing."

Wincing at the marshal's grip, Simpson released Hector's ear. "All right, Marshal," he spat as he twisted out of Travis's grasp. "The little troublemakers can go home. But I expect to see them in class tomorrow, and I promise you, they'll be given enough work to keep them out of trouble for years to come! Now, I have to get back to my students."

With that, he turned and stalked away.

Judging from the number of children among the crowd, Travis felt sure that Simpson was going to be upset when he returned to the schoolhouse and discovered that most of his charges had taken advantage of the opportunity to slip away from the school. That was Simpson's worry, though, not his.

Travis looked at Palmer and Aileen and shook his head. "Simpson's not too pleasant a fellow, is he?" he said.

"I'd like to get him up on the trapeze and be the one catching him—with no net below," Palmer commented dryly.

Travis grinned back at him, and then, like everyone else, turned to watch as the roof of the warehouse collapsed with a roar.

III

Thurman Simpson pushed his fingers through his thinning, dishwater-blond hair and sighed wearily. He surveyed the sullen faces of the children in the classroom, and his jaw tightened. It was nearly noon now, and it had taken him this long to round up enough of the students to continue with the day's work. Simpson wished he had never left the school to see what had caused the commotion earlier.

"All right," he said sharply as he leaned forward, palms flat on his desk. "Since we've already lost so much of the day, we shall have to make up some of the time by skipping our lunch period." He held up a hand to stifle the groans of protest. "Those of

52

you who have food with you may eat it at your desks, but I warn you! Not one crumb do I want to see on these floors, do you understand? Those of you who intended to go home to eat, well, perhaps next time you won't be so quick to try to take advantage of your teacher." Simpson's thin lips curved in what passed for a smile.

He knew he was being harsh on them, but it was what the little ingrates deserved, he thought. After all the time and effort he had spent trying to drum some education into their miserable brains, he was entitled to some respect.

"Now," he said, picking up the thin willow switch that he used as a pointer and turning to a map tacked on the wall, "we shall drill for an hour on the state and territorial capitals."

Simpson ignored the moans and groans and launched into the lesson. He had covered all of this so many times that he could recite the material in his sleep by now. As he forced them to repeat the capitals by rote, his mind began to wander.

His eyes moved around the large, single-room schoolhouse. Every desk was full, and some students were sitting on the floor in several places. There had been more than enough students for one teacher before that meddling nun and her orphans had arrived. Now Abilene's school was packed to bursting.

Thurman Simpson vividly remembered Sister Laurel's first visit. He had just finished giving a hiding to that obnoxious young Fields boy, and the lad was still sobbing as he tried to sit down at his desk. Sister Laurel had paused just inside the door of the school, frowning as she glanced at the little ruffian.

"Mr. Simpson?" she had asked, looking back at the teacher.

Simpson had return the frown. He never liked to be interrupted, especially by a woman. "Yes?" he had snapped. "What can I do for you, madam?"

"I'm Sister Laurel, Mr. Simpson," the nun had answered quietly as she moved into the room. "Perhaps you've heard that I recently arrived in Abilene with a group of orphans under my care."

"I have heard talk to that effect," Simpson had admitted. "But it's none of my affair."

Sister Laurel had paused, a tight smile on her face. "Oh, but it is now," she had said. "I've come to enroll the children in your school."

Simpson had shaken his head before the words were out of her mouth. "Out of the question. I already have too many students. You'll have to see to the education of your . . . orphans." He had somehow made the word sound dirty.

"But that's impossible," Sister Laurel had said over the excited babble that had come from the children in the room. "I'm not qualified to teach them, sir. That's your job."

"No, it is not, madam," Simpson had said stiffly.

"Mr. Simpson, the children at the orphanage are citizens of Abilene now and are entitled to the fine education Abilene offers in its schools," Sister Laurel replied, her blue eyes steadily measuring him.

Simpson's lip had curled. "This is *my* school."

"I was under the impression that you were appointed by the school board and that your salary was paid by the town," she had countered, warming to the argument.

"So it is. But I make the rules, and I say that the class is already full. So there you have it." He had drawn himself up to his full height, which was approximately the same as the woman's. "And now we must return to our work. There have been enough distractions for one day."

Sister Laurel had nodded toward the Fields boy, who was shifting uncomfortably in his seat, tears still running down his cheeks. "I suppose that poor boy caused a *distraction*."

"Indeed he did. And he was punished for it."

"I see," she had said. "Yes, I see it all. I wish you good day, Mr. Simpson." She had cast a sympathetic look at the Fields boy as she left the schoolroom shaking her head.

Thinking about what had happened as a result of the nun's visit was a bitter pill for Simpson to swallow.

The next morning right after the class had settled into its first lesson, Mr. Simpson had turned from the blackboard to see Sister Laurel at the schoolroom door. She had swept to the front of the room with over a dozen boys and girls of every age and description following in her wake and turned to the class with a radiant smile.

"Good morning, class. I've come to introduce your new classmates to you. This is Michael—"

"Oh, no you don't," Thurman Simpson had roared, cutting her off. "We have no room in this class. I told you that yesterday. As the schoolmaster, I will accept no more students—"

"And so you did, Mr. Simpson," Sister Laurel had agreed sweetly, cutting him off as effectively as he had her. "But perhaps you did not take everything into account when you made your decision. If you would be so good as to step outside for a moment." She had gestured graciously toward the door.

Every child in the room had sat motionless and wide-eyed, staring at the contest of wills being played out in front of them. As Mr. Simpson had strode past them to the back of the room, they had turned in their seats to watch him, the spunkier among them leaping to the windows as soon as he was outside.

The head of the school board and the mayor had stood in the school yard and told him in no uncertain terms that he would accept the orphans as students in the school.

"I tell you, I can't," Simpson had objected. "The school has too many students now. I'm only one man; I can't handle all of those . . . those little hooligans!"

The mayor had just glared at him. "You can if you expect to keep on getting paid, Simpson. Sister Laurel is a good friend of our new marshal, and besides, she's got a point. Those youngsters have just as much right to attend school here as any of the other children."

Simpson had stiffened his spine. "Perhaps you'd prefer to find a new teacher," he had said, confident that such would not be the case. There had been several teachers in Abilene before him, but he had been the only one strong enough not to be intimidated by the more obstinate pupils.

The mayor had nodded. "It will be a chore, all right, but we'll do it if we have to."

With that, Simpson's last bit of leverage had been gone. He was comfortable in Abilene, and he did not want to have to find a new job at this stage of his life. If the town was willing to fire him, there was nothing he could do but accept the newcomers into the school—albeit reluctantly.

Since that time, his resentment had grown to mammoth proportions. They were taking advantage of him, and he despised it. His workload had increased drastically, and Sister Laurel was trying to undermine everything he did. Every time he took the switch to one of the orphans, that infernal woman would show up at lunch recess the next day with cookies and punch for the entire class. Then she would lead them in songs and games. Those youngsters would race all over the school yard, laughing and yelling—and turning his well-ordered world into mayhem. It was impossible to make them settle down for the rest of the afternoon—and to make matters worse—his switch would have disappeared! It was obvious that woman had never spent time in a classroom and knew nothing about what was required to keep order.

As promised, Simpson continued the lesson on through the lunch hour. Several of the children who had not brought food with them were starting to fidget from hunger, but Simpson snapped at them and told them to keep still. He smiled as he slapped the top of his desk with the switch.

There was something about a schoolroom, he thought, something in the smell of chalk and sawdust that represented the things he valued most—control and power. In this room his word was law.

As if to undermine that thought, the door at the side of the room opened then, and Sister Laurel appeared. "Good afternoon, Mr. Simpson," she said with a smile.

Simpson suppressed a groan of dismay

and glared at the Dominican nun in her black habit. "Yes?" he said in an icy voice.

Sister Laurel moved into the room, the smile still on her face. Simpson knew from experience how deceptive that pleasant expression was. The nun asked, "Have you heard about the circus, Mr. Simpson?"

"Indeed I have. I saw one of those garish posters on a wall. It's a lot of foolishness, if you ask me."

The children knew about the circus, too, as Simpson was all too aware. Now, as Sister Laurel brought up the subject again, a wave of excited chatter swept the schoolroom.

Sister Laurel paused at the harshness of Simpson's tone, then drew a deep breath and plunged ahead. "I'm told that the arrival of the circus in the morning will be marked by a parade down Texas Street. Such a parade would be a wonderful educational experience for the children!"

One of the orphans, a boy with tousled red hair, let out a whoop of approval at the idea. Simpson spun to face the class and lashed the switch down on the desk with a sharp crack. "Hirsch!" he exclaimed. "Control yourself, boy! That outburst will cost you some extra work."

Sister Laurel shot a warning glance at Michael Hirsch. She knew quite well how rambunctious the young man could be, and he might wind up in even worse trouble if he responded to Simpson's threat. Michael slumped in his chair and contented himself with an angry stare at the teacher.

Simpson turned his attention back to Sister Laurel. "Your idea is impossible," he said shortly.

"But the children would enjoy it so. And it would give them the opportunity to see some exotic animals the likes of which they might never see again," Sister Laurel pointed out.

Simpson sniffed. "If they want to waste their time and money on such things, then let them finagle their parents into taking them to one of the performances. I simply will not dismiss school for such foolishness."

The nun looked at him for a long moment. "That's your final decision?" she said at last.

"Yes," Simpson said flatly. "My final decision."

Sister Laurel sighed deeply, shook her head, and left the schoolhouse without saying anything else.

Simpson faced his students once more and

saw with dismay the anger and resentment on their young faces. He was staring at open rebellion, and he knew it. There was only one way to deal with such a problem, and that was to meet it head on.

Simpson's lips drew back from his teeth in a grimace, and he said in a voice dripping with scorn, "If any of you think for one minute that you're not coming to class tomorrow, you can banish that notion from your heads. You *will* be here, even if I have to go to every one of your parents and explain the situation to them." He crossed his arms over his narrow chest. "You know your parents will agree with me."

That was his ace in the hole, he thought, to use an expression he considered crude but apt. Many of Abilene's parents approved of the way he taught and the methods he used to maintain discipline. This was a God-fearing, Bible-believing community, Simpson knew; there was little sparing of the rod around here.

A sullen silence settled over the room. For the moment, things were under control again, and Simpson intended to see that they stayed that way. "Now," he said, "we shall return to our work."

As the afternoon wore on, however, the

atmosphere of revolt grew. More and more of the students talked out of turn, and none of them seemed to know the correct answers when Simpson called on them, even the ones who could usually be depended upon. Even the best-behaved students, the ones who never gave him any trouble, wanted very badly to see the circus parade.

For the briefest of moments, Simpson considered changing his mind, but he quickly rejected that alternative. He was in charge here, and the children would simply have to accept his decision and get on with their work.

Simpson stood stiffly behind his desk and asked, "What do we know about the Louisiana Purchase?"

A rude sound came from the other side of the room, and Simpson looked quickly in that direction. He was met with blank looks, as if none of the students had heard the horrible noise, though several of them were trying very hard not to grin.

Redheaded Michael Hirsch was the first one to break. A laugh welled out of him, and he had to look away from Simpson's furious face.

"Michael Hirsch!" Simpson shouted. "Was that you who made that noise?"

Michael tried to control his laughter as he replied, "Noise? I thought that was you talking about the Louisiana Purchase, Mr. Simpson."

Simpson's fist clenched on the switch as more laughter swept across the room. They were making sport of him, and he would not stand for that.

He tried to forge on with the history lesson, but it was no use. Michael had created an opening, and the boy exploited it for all it was worth. For a change, he volunteered to answer questions, but none of his answers were correct. More noises came from other parts of the room as the courage of the other students grew.

And it was all the fault of that damned orphan, Simpson thought feverishly. Michael Hirsch was the instigator of this revolt.

Simpson had learned his own history lessons well, and he knew the best way to crush a revolt was to crush its leader. When he asked for volunteers to explain the purpose of the Lewis and Clark expedition, Michael's hand shot into the air. "I know!" the boy said without waiting to be called upon. "They were going to see the circus!"

A howl of approval went up from the children.

That was the last straw. Simpson's control snapped, and he lunged around the desk, his face contorted with rage. "Shut up!" he screamed, slashing at Michael with the switch.

Michael reacted quickly, dropping out of his seat in a dive to the side. A shocked silence fell over the classroom as Simpson continued to strike at him with the switch. Terror on his face, Michael darted away, heading for the door as the switch cut the air inches behind his head. Fumbling for the knob, he yanked the door open and lunged through. Simpson was after him in an instant.

Michael was fast and could outrun Simpson, but fate conspired against him. His foot caught on one of the roots of the tree that shaded the school yard, and he sprawled hard on his stomach in the dirt. Simpson was on him in a flash, lost in his fury. The teacher grabbed Michael's arm and jerked him painfully to his feet. The other hand lifted the switch, ready to administer a brutal hiding. The switch started to lash downward.

Fingers like iron came out of nowhere

and clamped around Simpson's wrist, stopping his arm before it had moved six inches.

Simpson gasped in pain and jerked his head around to see who had grabbed him. He found himself staring into the dark, angry eyes of Deputy Cody Fisher.

Coolly, Cody said, "Why don't you take that switch after me if you're of a mind to hit somebody?"

"I—I—" Simpson stammered.

" 'Course, I expect I'd hit you back," Cody continued. A humorless grin stretched across his face. "Now, let that kid go."

Simpson released Michael's arm as if it were a hot coal. "You—you've got no right to interfere, Deputy," he said, trying to keep his voice from quivering.

"Maybe not, but I'm glad I was passing by anyway." Cody glanced down at the red-headed orphan. "What's this all about, Michael?"

The boy brushed some of the dirt from his twill pants. "Aw, we just wanted to go see the circus parade tomorrow, and Mr. Simpson says we've got to go to school instead."

Cody's grin was genuine now. "So you young hellions tried to make him see the error of his ways."

Michael smiled sheepishly. "Something like that, yeah."

Cody turned back to the angry teacher and released Simpson's wrist. Simpson started to massage the aching limb, but then pride made him stop.

Cody said, "Sounds reasonable enough to me that the kids want to go to the parade, Mr. Simpson. They could learn a lot about animals and things like that."

Simpson glared at the deputy. "I've been over all this with that . . . that nun," he sputtered. "The decision is mine to make, and I say that I will not dismiss school for such frivolity."

Simpson glanced past the young man and saw the students crowding around the windows in the schoolhouse, taking in everything that was happening. It would strengthen his position greatly, Simpson thought, if he demonstrated that he would not back down from Cody.

Suddenly, Cody smiled again. "I've got it," he said proudly. "Sister Laurel and I will go see the mayor and ask him if he'll declare tomorrow a school holiday. He is your boss, right, Mr. Simpson?"

Simpson knew how the mayor could be browbeaten into accepting anything that nun and this gunslinging lawman might ask. There was a sick taste of defeat in his mouth as he admitted, "I am employed by the town. And I suppose you're right, Deputy. The parade . . . could prove educational. I suppose the children could attend—as a school trip of sorts."

Realizing that he and the other children had won, Michael let out a whoop of triumph. As the celebration spread rapidly, the uproar inside the schoolhouse threatened to raise the roof.

Cody slapped Simpson on the shoulder. "Glad you saw it my way, Mr. Simpson," he said.

The teacher glared at him. "I intend to report this interference to the marshal, Fisher. I still say you've got no right to meddle in school affairs."

"You go right ahead," Cody told him. The deputy reached out and ruffled Michael's hair. "Back inside, kid. You've still got some studying to do."

Michael nodded. "All right, Cody." The hero worship was plain in his eyes.

Simpson started to turn toward the school and follow Michael inside, but Cody stopped him. Cody plucked the switch from the hands of the surprised teacher, and before

Simpson could stop him, he had snapped the weapon in two.

"You can tell the marshal about *that*, too," Cody said. He walked away, leaving the dumbfounded Simpson staring after him.

IV

Ned Cahoon, Mitch Stark, and Hack Dawson rode back into Abilene an hour after sunset. Although none of them would have admitted it, they had waited this long to return so that their chance of running into Marshal Luke Travis would be lessened.

There was a bruise on Cahoon's wrist where Travis had knocked the gun from his hand and a swelling on his jaw where the marshal's hard fist had landed. Cahoon's brow was knitted in a frown as he pulled his horse to a stop in front of Orion's Tavern.

Slender, rabbit-faced Mitch Stark nervously ran a hand over his jaw. "You don't reckon Travis will be in there, do you, Ned?" he asked.

Cahoon snorted derisively. "I don't care if he is. He took me by surprise this morning, but if that damned star-packer tries anything with me again, I'll be ready for him."

Hack Dawson, who was blond and stocky and appeared more suited for clerking in a hardware store than running with a group of hardcases, gave a gusty sigh. "That's easy to say, Cahoon," he pointed out. "But that fella Travis has got himself quite a reputation. He ain't going to be easy to take down."

Cahoon jerked around to face his companion. "You shut up, Dawson!" he snapped. "I didn't notice you pitchin' in this morning."

"I wasn't looking to get shot, you mean."

Cahoon made no reply to that. He swung down from the saddle and grabbed at the hitch rail to steady himself as he swayed a little. The three young men had been sitting under a tree all day, waiting for night to fall, and had polished off two bottles of whiskey from their saddlebags. Ned Cahoon had consumed more than his share of the liquor, but he believed he could handle it.

Now, their whiskey gone, they had returned to Abilene to have a few more drinks and buy a bottle to take with them. As he stepped onto the boardwalk in front of the tavern, Cahoon thrust a hand in the pocket of his pants and tried to determine by feel how much money remained there. He handled the money for all three of them, not because he was better with finances than Stark or Dawson, but because the other two were afraid of him and he knew it. That was the way it should be, he had often thought. He was the leader because he was the strongest, the most dangerous.

The three of them had been together for several years, working as cowhands on the trail drives coming up from Texas. It was hard, dirty, low-paying work, but it was all they knew how to do. Every summer they helped push a couple of herds up to Kansas, blew what little pay they earned in Abilene, and then drifted back to Texas to scrounge through another winter.

The previous summer, Ned Cahoon had talked them into changing that pattern. He had persuaded his two companions to remain in Kansas with him, convinced that their opportunities would be better here.

At first, that had not been the case. The winter had been just as hard, money just as scarce as ever. They had been broke when they rode up to a small farmhouse west of Abilene hoping to cadge a hot meal.

That was the day they had crossed the line into lawlessness.

When Cahoon saw that the young, attractive woman was there alone, he had known what was going to happen. New to the frontier, she made the mistake of admitting that her husband had gone into Abilene and would not be back for hours.

It had been a long, pleasurable afternoon once she stopped screaming and fighting and accepted the inevitable. And while Stark and Dawson were taking their turns with her, Cahoon had found a cache of bills in the sugar jar. It was enough money to tide them over for several weeks.

He had been thinking of killing the woman before they left so that she could not set the law on them, but Dawson and Stark had talked him out of it. Later he had discovered that the woman had dug out the pistol her husband had left with her—the gun that she should have had loaded and ready—and had blown her own brains out with it. That was good luck, Cahoon had thought. Good luck followed a man who was not afraid to take chances.

From that moment on he had decided that when he wanted something, he was going to take it.

So far, they had been lucky. They had looted several other farmhouses and had even pulled off a daylight robbery in Hayes City. They had been masked, and no one had gotten a good look at them. In fact, there were no wanted posters out on them at all, so they were free to come and go as they pleased.

Of course, they had never again come across a situation like that first one, and Cahoon regretted that. That young wife had been mighty sweet. . . .

The sight of one of the circus posters on the wall of the tavern drove that pleasant memory out of Cahoon's head. Twisting his lips in a snarl, he strode to the poster, ripped the handbill from the wall, and crumpled it.

"Goddamn circus!" he said as he flung the wadded-up poster into the street. "It was that crippled bastard's fault!"

"Yeah," Stark agreed. "We was just funnin' him. The marshal had no right to butt in like that."

"Come on," Dawson said. "I want another drink." With Cahoon in the lead, the three of them pushed through the swinging batwing doors.

Orion's establishment was doing a good business this evening. There were poker games going on at a couple of the tables, and most of the others were filled with men drinking and talking. Several more men were standing at the long mahogany bar that ran down one side of the room. The candles in the chandeliers cast a warm yellow glow over the place.

The burly redbearded proprietor was serving as his own bartender. Placing his palms flat on the bar, he regarded the three newcomers with suspicious eyes. "What'll ye boys be having?" Orion asked.

Cahoon slouched against the bar. "Whiskey, for all of us," he ordered.

Orion nodded, took three glasses from a shelf on the back bar, and picked up a bottle.

Cahoon stopped him by saying, "Is that the good stuff, McCarthy?"

Narrowing his eyes, Orion rumbled in reply, "All the stuff, as ye put it, is good in me bar."

"Aye, the good stuff! The good stuff!"

Cahoon's head jerked up at the sound of the shrill voice. He spotted the brightly colored parrot sitting on its perch on the backbar. With a scowl, he said, "Somebody's goin' to make stew out of that damned bird one of these days, McCarthy."

"Stew out o' Old Bailey?" Orion laughed shortly. "Dinna be daft, man. 'Twould take a heap o' cookin' t'soften up tha' stringy old devil!"

"Dinna be daft, man!" the parrot squawked. "Dinna be daft!"

Mitch Stark put his hand on the butt of his gun. "Bet I could make some feathers fly," he said with a grin.

Orion poured whiskey into the three glasses, and as he shoved Stark's glass toward him, he said, "Take ye hand off ye gun, mister. There'll be none o' tha' in this establishment." The tavern keeper's voice was hard and cold.

"Ah, hell," Stark muttered. "I was just jokin'." He moved his hand away from the butt of the pistol.

As Orion put the cork back in the bottle, Cahoon reached out to wrap his fingers around its neck. "We'll take the bottle, too," he said.

"Ye'll pay for it first," Orion shot back.

Cahoon grunted, tossed off the liquor in his glass, then dug into his pocket and produced several coins. Slapping them down on the bar, he turned toward one of the few empty tables, taking the bottle with him. Dawson and Stark followed along behind.

They settled down for some serious drinking, Cahoon doing the pouring. The three of them spoke very little, concentrating instead on the liquor and on the cigarettes they rolled."

Cahoon was aware that several people in the room glanced at him, but that was what he wanted. Famous outlaws attracted attention; that was his goal. One of these days the Cahoon gang would be just as well known as the James boys or the Reno brothers. As the leader of the daring band, people would respect him—and fear him.

As he listened to the conversations going on around him, though, he became aware that no one was talking about him. Instead, everyone was talking about the impending arrival of Professor Jericho Jeffries's Traveling Circus and Extravaganza.

Cahoon's expression became more and more sour as he overheard the excited discussion of the circus's attractions. He tossed down his drinks faster, and the level of whiskey in the bottle dropped rapidly.

His friends were listening to the talk, too, and finally Mitch Stark leaned forward and asked in a voice that sounded almost as intrigued as a child's, "Are we goin' to the circus, Ned?"

"Why the hell would we do that?" Cahoon growled. "Circuses are for kids, Stark."

"Oh, I don't know," Dawson said. "I think it sounds like it might be fun. You're just mad because the cripple landed a punch on you, Ned."

Cahoon's fingers tightened on his glass. "He was just as lucky as Travis. I'll teach him a lesson if I ever run into him again."

Dawson sipped his drink. "You might see him at the circus if we went," he suggested.

Slowly, Cahoon nodded. He had not considered that possibility.

Sensing that Cahoon was wavering in his decision, Stark said quickly, "I hear they've got this pretty gal who's a sharpshooter, Ned. Wouldn't you like to see that?"

Cahoon laughed. His voice becoming louder, he said, "Hell, no woman can shoot as good as a man."

"She's supposed to be good," Dawson added, repeating what he had heard from the table behind him.

Cahoon stared into his drink and brooded for a moment, then finished off the whiskey. As he banged the glass back down on the table, he declared, "I say no woman can outshoot me!" Lifting his voice even more, he continued. "And I dare any man in this saloon to deny it!"

"Here now, mister," a cowboy at a nearby table spoke up. "There's no call to get upset."

Cahoon fixed him with a glare. "I'm not upset. I just don't want anybody thinkin' some female can outshoot me." He pushed his chair back, the legs scraping on the plank floor. "And I don't like you sayin' she can."

The cowboy held up his hands. "Hell, I didn't say that. I don't even know how you can shoot."

Cahoon faced the man, his hands hanging loose at his sides, the fingers almost brushing the butts of the two guns he wore. In a soft voice, he said, "Why don't you find out?"

Silence fell over the big room as the patrons realized what was about to happen. The surprised cowboy swallowed anxiously. "I ain't no gunfighter, mister," he said.

"You sure as hell were fast enough with your mouth," Cahoon grated.

Behind him at the table, Stark and Dawson exchanged glances. Cahoon could always be counted on for some fun when he had been boozing, even if it was just putting the run on some poor dumb puncher.

The cowboy said, "I never meant no offense. I just wanted to go see that circus when it comes to town."

Cahoon took a deep breath and controlled his anger. "You just do that," he told the cowboy. "You go see that gal who's supposed to be so damn good with a gun. You'll see. I'll prove she's nothin'." Cahoon cast his stormy gaze around the room. "You'll all see!"

Several men were muttering angrily now as Cahoon glared at them. A few pushed back their chairs, ready to get up and take issue with his drunken boasting. The feel of a brawl was in the air, and Cahoon, for one, would be only too glad to bust some heads.

"All right," Orion said from the bar, his heavy voice cutting through the tension in the room. "Tha' is enough, I'm thinking. Ye and ye friends had best leave, bucko."

Cahoon spun toward the bar, his hand going to his gun. Before he could draw it, Hack Dawson lunged across the table, reaching out frantically. As he caught Cahoon's wrist and held it there, the Colt undrawn, he warned, "No, Ned! Don't do it!"

Cahoon started to curse his friend bitterly, but then he saw why Dawson had acted as he had. Orion McCarthy held a shotgun in his big hands, and the double barrels were staring right at him. He had not noticed the click of both barrels being cocked, but there was no doubt about it; they were ready to fire.

Suddenly, Cahoon sneered. "You touch off that scattergun in here, old man, and you'll blast half your customers along with me. That what you want?"

Men at the tables surrounding Cahoon scattered. Chairs overturned as they were hastily vacated.

"Maybe I'll hit 'em 'n' maybe I won't," Orion said. "But ye won't know about it if I do, Cahoon, 'cause ye'll be cut in half by this buckshot."

The parrot screeched, "Cut in half! Aye, cut in half!"

Mitch Stark was pale and sweating, and Hack Dawson kept glancing nervously at Orion. Dawson released Cahoon's wrist and muttered, "Forget it, Ned. It ain't worth it."

Cahoon looked at them, contempt plain on his features. "What the hell good are you?" he snapped. "You two won't even back up a partner!"

Dawson shook his head, stood up, and moved away from the table. "I just don't want to get killed over something like this,

Ned. That circus ain't worth it, and neither is some sharpshooting girl."

A long moment went by. Cahoon saw how rock-steady the barrels of the shotgun were, and finally he took a deep breath and moved his hand away from his gun. "All right," he growled. "But I won't forget this, McCarthy."

"I dinna care if ye forget or not, lad," Orion said. "Just so ye get out o' me tavern."

Cahoon turned sharply away and stalked to the door, pushing past Dawson. Stark stood up hurriedly, and along with Dawson, they followed Cahoon.

Cahoon paused at the batwings and looked back at the patrons of the saloon. "I meant what I said," he told them. "All of you bastards go to your damn circus. You'll see me teach that bitch a thing or two about shootin'!"

Then he was gone, pushing out through the batwings into the night, his companions on his heels.

Luke Travis was at his desk, flipping through the latest bunch of wanted posters he had received, when he heard the thump of booted feet on the boardwalk outside. As he glanced up, the door of his office opened, and Orion McCarthy's burly frame moved through the entrance.

" 'Evening, Orion," Travis said, squaring the sheaf of reward-dodgers and placing them in one of the desk drawers. "What are you doing out and about at this hour? I'd think you'd be behind your bar now, pouring drinks."

Orion waved a big hand. "Ah, I left the place wi' one o' the lads for a short time. 'Twas talkin' to ye I thought I should be doin'."

"Then have a seat." Travis nodded at the chair on the other side of the desk. "Is there a problem down at the tavern?"

Orion snorted as he sat down heavily. "Don't run across too many problems I kinna handle, Lucas. 'Tis worried about someone else, I am. Ye know a young fella, name o' Ned Cahoon?"

"Cahoon?" Travis said with a frown. The name was familiar, but . . . Then it came back to him. That was the name of the cowboy who had picked the fight with Gil Palmer that morning, before the warehouse fire. "Sure, I know him," the marshal went on. "In fact, now that I think about it, I've heard some talk that he and some of his friends may be behind some of the robberies we've had in the area lately. Have Cahoon and his bunch been bothering you?"

Orion's bearded face was wreathed in a grin. "Ye know this Scotsman, Lucas. If I was worried about Ned Cahoon, I'd be handling it meself. He was in me place a bit ago, drinkin' too much, o' course, 'n' he near started a brawl. Lookin' down the barrels o' me shotgun changed his mind for him."

"It doesn't surprise me that he was causing trouble," Travis commented. "I had to kick him out of town this morning when he tried to rough up a stranger. What was it about tonight?"

"He was mad about that circus comin' t'town, he was. He said he was ginna show that female sharpshooter that she could'na outshoot him."

Travis frowned. "This morning Cahoon had a run-in with the fellow putting up handbills to advertise the circus. It sounds like he's holding a grudge against the whole show."

Orion tapped the side of his head with a blunt finger and said, "I'm thinking young Cahoon's a wee bit off in the head, Lucas."

Travis nodded. He leaned back in his chair and frowned thoughtfully. "I figured this circus would bring trouble to town with it." The marshal paused, then went on, "Well, we'll just wait and see. If any trouble comes up, we'll handle it. I know one thing—I plan to be keeping a close eye on Professor Jericho Jeffries and his performers. I'll watch out for Cahoon, too. Maybe we can head off any trouble before it starts."

Even as he said it, his lawman's instincts told him that was not the way things were going to work out.

V

Even though the circus was not to arrive until later in the morning, the crowds began to gather not long after the sun came up the next day. As Luke Travis leaned on the railing of the boardwalk in front of the marshal's office, with Cody Fisher beside him, he watched the steady stream of traffic into Abilene and shook his head.

"Looks like word of the circus got around all over these parts," Cody commented.

Travis nodded. "Plenty of folks coming in from the country, all right."

There were wagons and buckboards and buggies tied up all along the street. Whole families had come in from the farms and ranches in the surrounding area. Children ran here and there, laughing excitedly, unable to contain the anticipation they felt. Most of the shops along Texas Street opened early and were already doing a brisk business.

Travis glanced down the boardwalk and saw the attractive, dark-haired form of Dr. Aileen Bloom approaching. He smiled at her and touched the brim of his hat, and Cody did likewise. "Good morning," Travis said. "Have you turned out for the parade, too, Aileen?"

"As a matter of fact, that's why I'm here," Aileen replied as she returned the marshal's smile. "I thought it would be a good idea to be on hand in case there were any injuries. And I must admit, the idea of seeing the parade itself is exciting."

"I hope your medical services aren't needed."

"Well, I'll be here in case they are." Aileen rested her hands on the boardwalk railing and looked out at the crowd in the street. "My, there's certainly quite a turnout."

"Half the folks in Kansas and three fourths of the dogs," Cody said with a grin.

Aileen laughed softly. Travis divided his attention between the street and the doctor, thinking that Aileen was certainly looking lovely today. She was wearing a lightweight cotton frock, and her lustrous brunette hair was piled atop her head in appealing curls. She was about as far from the common conception of a doctor as could be. Since her mentor, Dr. Levi Wright, had gone into retirement, Aileen had handled the medical needs of the community and done an excellent job of it. Travis thought Abilene was lucky to have her.

"Ah, good mornin' t'ye," Orion McCarthy called from down the block, lifting a big hand in greeting. He joined the little group in front of the marshal's office.

"You're up early this morning, Orion," Travis said. "It couldn't be that you've come to watch the circus parade, too?"

"I'll not deny it, Lucas. 'Twill be quite a spectacle, I expect."

Travis nodded. "It should be a while yet before the circus arrives. Why don't we go in the office and have some coffee while we wait?"

The others agreed. Travis had put a pot of coffee on to brew as soon as he arrived at the office, and by now it was ready.

As the four of them settled down in chairs to sip the strong black liquid, Orion asked, "Have ye seen anything o' tha' young fellow' Cahoon this morning, Lucas?"

As Travis shook his head, Cody exclaimed, "Cahoon? Is he causing trouble again, Marshal?"

"He was running his mouth off in me tavern last evening, laddie," Orion said. "Claimed he was ginna cause trouble for them circus folk, he did."

Travis said quietly, "Cahoon's more talk than he is action. He'll back down anytime the odds aren't heavily in his favor."

"We'd better keep an eye out for him anyway," Cody said dubiously. "I never have trusted him."

When they had finished their coffee, Travis stood up and said, "Cody, you and I had better take a turn around town. Aileen, you and Orion feel free to wait here in the office if you want to."

"All right," Aileen replied. "If anyone comes in looking for you, we'll tell them you'll be back shortly."

"Thanks." Travis nodded.

Together, he and Cody left the office and began strolling down the boardwalk. Abilene was even more crowded now, Travis saw.

Everybody who lived anywhere near town had come in, and many of the bystanders called greetings to the two lawmen.

Travis and Cody took their time, ambling up one side of Texas Street and then down the other, pausing to chat with several of the merchants and many of the spectators. By the time the two men returned to the marshal's office, Aileen and Orion had moved outside and were sitting on a couple of the wooden chairs that lined the boardwalk next to the wall of the building. Travis and Cody joined them.

Orion pulled a massive watch from his pants pocket and opened it. "Near eleven o'clock," he grunted. "They ought t'be here soon."

"I hope so," Travis said. "Folks are getting a little restless."

Suddenly a cheer went up, far down the street to the east. The cry was taken up and passed along through the crowd.

"Must be them," Aileen said with a grin.

Travis stood up, stepped off the boardwalk, and walked into the center of the street, peering to the east. Dust was rising just on the edge of town, and Travis could hear faint strains of music above the bustle around him.

"You folks, clear the street," he called to the bystanders. "Everybody up on the boardwalks!"

Travis rejoined his friends in front of the office. The four of them leaned on the railing and peered to the east.

From across the street, someone called Cody's name. The deputy glanced up to see Michael Hirsch standing on the opposite boardwalk with a group of the students from the school. Thurman Simpson was standing behind them, glaring across the street. Clearly he had not forgotten the incident with Cody the day before.

Michael waved excitedly, and Cody returned the wave. Noticing the exchange, Travis leaned over to his deputy and said, "I hope Simpson can keep those kids in line. I don't want any of them running out into the street and getting hurt."

"They're good kids," Cody replied. "They won't get into trouble."

Cody grinned at the memory of his confrontation with the teacher. Obviously, Simpson had not gone to Travis with his complaints, or Cody would have heard about it from the marshal. "When does that old sourpuss ever look happy?" he asked. Travis chuckled and did not answer.

The music came plainly to their ears now, traditional marching tunes designed to stir the hearts of young and old alike. The circus band came into sight, the music blending with the cheers of the crowd. Wearing white pants, bright red jackets, and plumed hats, the band would have looked like a military unit except for their carrying instruments instead of weapons. It was not a large band, perhaps a dozen men, but they played with an enthusiasm that belied their size.

Following the band came the first of the circus wagons, its sides boldly emblazoned with the legend PROFESSOR JERICHO JEFFRIES'S TRAVELING CIRCUS AND EXTRAVAGANZA. Four beautiful white stallions wearing silver-studded harnesses pulled the wagon. Atop the seat stood a man dressed in white trousers tucked into high black boots and a brilliant crimson jacket with long tails. On his head was a black top hat, which he doffed frequently to the crowd. He was tall and broad-shouldered, and his dark, neatly trimmed beard was shot with gray.

"Hello!" he called to the bystanders as the wagon rolled past. "Good to see you! Be sure to come to the circus!"

Professor Jericho Jeffries himself, Travis

thought, studying the thoroughly distinguished gentleman.

Behind the professor's wagon came several men in gaudy coats, garish makeup, and shoes several sizes too large. Laughter ran through the crowd at the sight of the clowns. Maintaining their rather solemn demeanor, the clowns raised battered hats in greeting, then proceeded to trip over their own feet. One of them took several brightly colored wooden balls from the pocket of his oversized jacket and began juggling them, keeping up the dizzying routine for several seconds before he allowed one of the balls to bounce off his head. That provoked more laughter from the children.

Another wagon featured several men and women in tight, spangled costumes waving to the crowd, and Travis knew they had to be the acrobats—*aerialists*, Gil Palmer had called them. Travis wondered where Palmer was this morning. He had not seen the man since the aftermath of the fire the day before.

A fresh surge of cries issued from the impressed spectators as they saw the trick riders coming down the street. There were two men and a woman, the men riding abreast on magnificent horses and the woman standing on the shoulders of the men.

"That don't look so hard," Cody muttered beside Travis as the trick riders passed by.

"I reckon you'd like to give it a try," Travis said.

"I just might," Cody replied confidently. "I was riding before I could walk, Marshal."

Orion reached across Travis and plucked Cody's sleeve. "Why dinna ye try a hand at tha' instead, laddie?" he asked as he pointed to the next attraction.

It was a barred wagon with two huge striped cats inside. Riding on top of the wagon was a handsome blond man in gold tights and a spangled jacket. Cody stared at the big cats and said, "Those are the funniest-looking mountain lions I ever did see."

Aileen laughed. "They're tigers, Cody. Bengal tigers from the country of India. Impressive, aren't they?"

Cody nodded and said, "Yes, ma'am, they are."

There were two more of the barred wagons, these containing lions, which Aileen explained came from Africa. It was obvious from the animated look on her face and the sound of her voice that she was enjoying herself. She was actually seeing things that until now she had seen only in books.

Travis nudged Cody. "What about them? Think you could ride one of those?"

He pointed at a pair of massive gray elephants. Small, dark-skinned men rode on the back of each animal. With their wrinkled skin, huge flapping ears, writhing snouts, and long curved tusks, the elephants provoked shouts of amazement as they plodded along Texas Street.

Cody swallowed as he regarded the elephants. "Reckon I can ride anything with four legs," he said bravely.

"Dinna be daft, man!" Orion exclaimed. "Them beasts would step on ye till there was naught left!"

Slapping the railing, Cody suddenly pointed. "There she is! There's the gal I've been waiting for!"

Riding a beautifully groomed, prancing horse, the young woman whose likeness adorned the posters rode past, wearing a buckskin dress glittering with fancy beadwork and a cream-colored Stetson atop her long chestnut hair. The smile she turned toward the spectators was dazzling. Around her hips was a shell belt supporting two holstered Colts, their ivory grips sparkling in the sunlight. In her hands she carried a presentation model Winchester, known as an Old Yellowboy.

For a moment she seemed to be smiling directly at Cody, and he let out a whoop of excitement.

"You still want to go with me when I ride out to talk to Jeffries later?" Travis asked dryly.

"Just try to stop me!" Cody shot back.

Travis grinned and shook his head.

There were more wagons being driven by roustabouts, and then came the sideshow performers, some of them walking, some on horseback. There were midgets and giants and a bearded lady that made Cody and Orion gawk. One man seemed to swallow a long sharp sword; another breathed flame like a dragon of legend. While one of the performers carried a long snake draped around his neck, another seemed to be completely covered with tattoos. And accompanying the members of the sideshow were more clowns, one of them riding a horse.

Travis glanced across the street. The faces of the schoolchildren were wreathed in big smiles, and their eyes were wide. Several were almost bouncing up and down on the

94

boardwalk in their excitement. This was obviously a high point in their young lives.

Thurman Simpson reached out and yanked one boy away from the railing when the youngster began leaning forward. He spoke sharply, his voice rising over the excited babble of the crowd as he told the children to stand still and behave themselves. His scolding seemed to have no effect.

The clown on horseback suddenly spotted the children and swerved his horse toward them. He reached into the pocket of his brightly checkered coat and pulled out a handful of penny candies. With a big grin on his face, he called, "Here you go, kiddies!" He began tossing the candy, one piece at a time, toward the children.

Shouting in their enthusiasm, the youngsters grabbed for the treats, and there was instant pandemonium on the boardwalk as they vied with one another for the candy. It was good-natured chaos, however.

Simpson did not see it that way, and he yelled, "Here now! Children, stop that! Stop it, I say!" The words fell on deaf ears.

Simpson's narrow features contorted in anger as he saw the last vestiges of his control slipping away. The obstinate little beasts were making a mockery of him, aided by that idiotically grinning clown.

"You there!" he shouted at the performer. "Stop that this instant! Stop it!"

The clown kept grinning and tossing candy, ignoring Simpson every bit as much as the children did.

Furious, Simpson pushed a couple of his students aside and stepped off the boardwalk into the street. In his hand was a willow switch, which he had cut that very morning as a replacement for the one Cody had destroyed. Shuddering with rage, he raised the switch and started toward the clown.

"I said stop it!"

The howl of anger from Simpson made the clown glance at him. Seeing the man approaching with the switch upraised, the clown jerked back on the reins in surprise. The horse he was riding, high-strung to start with, reacted instantly, spooking and rearing up on its hind legs.

Simpson stopped in his tracks as he saw the iron-shod hooves lashing out at him. He tried to step backward, but his feet became tangled, and he lost his balance. As Simpson sat down hard in the dust of the street, the rearing horse looming over him, a screech of fear tore from his throat.

Travis, hearing the frightened yell, glanced over in time to see the clown desperately trying to control his nervous mount. Someone was lying in the street, and Travis recognized him as Thurman Simpson. Shouting, "Come on!" to Cody, Travis vaulted the hitch rail and raced across the street, dodging a couple of scurrying midgets in ten-gallon hats on the way.

Simpson finally regained his wits enough to use his hands and feet to push himself backward toward the boardwalk. The clown reined in tightly and tried to calm the horse by speaking to it in a soothing voice. Several of the children shouted in fear as they saw their teacher in danger of being trampled, and a couple of the townsmen nearby jumped off the boardwalk and hurried to help.

When the men reached Simpson, each of them grabbed an arm and jerked him to his feet. He backpedaled frantically until he reached the boardwalk, where he tripped and sat down again. By this time, the clown's horse had stopped rearing, although it still sidled back and forth nervously. The crowd, which had fallen silent as it realized

Simpson's danger, now relaxed, and laughter began to sweep through the bystanders. Despite the potential seriousness of the situation, Simpson had looked pretty ludicrous.

Travis pushed through to Simpson's side. He took the teacher's arm and helped him to his feet. "Are you all right, Mr. Simpson?" Travis asked.

The teacher, shaking from a combination of fear, anger, and outraged dignity, pointed a quivering finger at the clown, who had finally calmed his mount. "That man tried to kill me!" Simpson charged.

From the back of the horse, the clown responded, "Hey, it was an accident, mister. You started it by coming at me and waving that switch around."

Realizing that he still held the switch in his hand, Simpson raised it again and took a step toward the clown, but Travis stopped him with a firm hand on his arm.

"Just hold on, Mr. Simpson," the marshal cautioned. "We don't want to start the trouble all over again."

"That horse is a menace!" Simpson said. "And so is that . . . that creature riding him! I demand that you arrest that man, Marshal, and I want the horse shot! I'd do it myself if I had my gun!"

A chorus of protests came from the schoolchildren, and the clown said grimly, "Nobody's shooting this horse, mister. It was your own fault he nearly stepped on you."

"My fault!" Simpson's eyes popped with amazement. "I was simply trying to control my students, who, I might add, were being worked into a frenzy by your irresponsible behavior, you lout!" The teacher swung toward Travis. "Marshal, are you going to act on my complaint or not?"

"Just take it easy, Mr. Simpson," Travis said, trying to calm the situation. "There doesn't seem to be any harm done, so why don't we just let the circus get on with its parade so that folks can enjoy themselves?"

"What?" Simpson's voice was shrill. He took a deep breath and visibly controlled himself. "You're not going to arrest that man or have his horse shot, are you, Marshal?"

Travis shook his head. "No, Mr. Simpson, I'm not."

"I see." Simpson glanced at Cody, who was standing nearby, grinning. "I was going to have a talk with you about the behavior of your deputy, Mr. Travis, but I see now that would have done no good, either. You ruffians are all alike. You have no respect for a man of learning!"

Travis's mouth was tight as he tried to control his own temper. "Sorry you feel that way, Mr. Simpson." He turned to the clown and jerked a thumb down the street. "You'd best get on with the rest of the parade, mister."

The clown nodded. "Thanks, Marshal." He urged the horse into a trot to catch up with the other clowns.

Travis and Cody left Simpson standing on the boardwalk with his students. The teacher glared after them as he brushed off his clothes.

Travis glanced at Cody as they crossed the street through an opening in the parade. "Why was Simpson going to have a talk with me about you?" he asked.

"Aw, hell, I just stopped him from whaling the tar out of young Michael Hirsch yesterday. It didn't amount to anything, Marshal."

"Well, you'd best steer clear of him for a while."

They rejoined Aileen and Orion on the boardwalk, and Travis quickly answered their questions about what had occurred across the street. "Was Mr. Simpson all right?" Aileen asked.

"Nothing hurt but his pride," Travis replied. "Unfortunately, in his case that's a pretty big injury."

They turned their attention back to the remainder of the parade, which was now winding down. More ranks of exotic animals came by. Travis recognized the camels, having seen them during the Army's ill-fated experiment with camels as cavalry mounts. Several zebras and some small apes—dressed in clothes as if they were human—strode by, and then a final group of clowns brought up the rear, along with several plain wagons piled high with supplies. The sound of the band had long since faded.

"Looks like that's it," Cody said, straightening from the railing. "Are we going to head out to their camp now, Marshal?" He sounded eager to get started.

"Let's let them get settled in a little first," Travis replied. "Don't worry, Cody. You'll get to see that sharpshooting gal soon enough."

Cody grinned. "When it comes to a pretty girl, Marshal, it's never soon enough."

VI

Travis and Cody ate lunch at the café, then saddled their horses and rode down Texas Street toward the western edge of town. Riding through the oldest section of Abilene, they passed the old saloon where Daddy Jones had sold prairie dogs to travelers, and the former Bratton Hotel, which despite its name had been just a six-room log cabin. As they crossed the Kansas Pacific railroad tracks, Travis told Cody of the famous observation made by an early visitor who claimed that Abilene was nothing but a muddy trail and half-dozen miserable hovels.

"No longer, marshal." Cody laughed. "This town has grown since then and so has our job. You know how much work we have."

As they rode past the last buildings to the edge of the prairie, the circus's camp stood less than a quarter of a mile away in sharp relief against the clear spring sky. In under two hours the performers and roustabouts had worked wonders. The brightly painted wagons were arranged in a rough half-circle.

Several small tents had been erected. All of the horses grazed in a makeshift corral; elephants and camels were tethered to stout stakes driven in the ground. *Bizarre*, thought Cody, looking at the elephants standing in the Kansas plain, as he and Travis rode past them into the camp.

People were hurrying everywhere. It was controlled chaos as the roustabouts and performers unloaded the wagons. In the center of a large open space, the canvas of the big top was being unrolled. The air was filled with the sound of sledgehammers pounding stakes into the hard earth. Elephants trumpeted, lions and tigers growled, and men shouted constantly.

Cody sat in his saddle and took in the confusion for a long moment, then said, "Incredible that they each know what they're doing!"

"Looks like most of them have been at it for a long time," Travis replied. "Come on, let's see if we can find the head man."

Travis walked his horse past a low ring being laid out by the trick riders. Cody followed behind him. Scanning the camp, Travis spotted the wagon that had led the parade and started toward it.

The man in the top hat and bright red

coat was standing beside the wagon, his hands clasped behind his back, rocking back and forth on his booted heels. He was surveying the activity with a look of satisfaction on his face. That expression changed to curiosity as he spotted Travis and Cody riding through the bustle toward him. When the lawmen reined in, the man stepped forward to greet them.

Travis swung down from the saddle. "Professor Jeffries?" he asked.

"Professor Jericho Jeffries, Marshal, owner of Professor Jericho Jeffries's Traveling Circus and Extravaganza, at your service. What can I do for you, sir?" He had a deep, rich voice that contained a trace of an English accent.

Travis extended his hand. As Jeffries shook it, the marshal said, "I'm Luke Travis, Abilene's marshal, and this is my deputy, Cody Fisher."

Jeffries shook hands with Cody as well and said, "Very pleased to meet you, Marshal. You, too, Deputy."

"We thought we'd better ride out and have a little talk with you, Professor Jeffries," Travis said. "I'm sure none of us want any problems during your visit."

Suspicion narrowed Jeffries's eyes. "This

isn't about that incident during the parade, is it? My clown has informed me that the citizen was at fault in the matter. We've had trouble with people like that before. I assure you, Marshal, this circus will not be a party to extortion. I won't give the man a penny."

Travis held up both hands. "Hold on a minute, Professor. I know the man who was involved pretty well, and I'm not blaming your performer at all. It was just an unfortunate incident, and no charges have been filed."

"Well, all right then." Jeffries sounded mollified. "If you're not here about that, what can I do for you?"

"I meant what I said about not wanting trouble," Travis told him bluntly. "Everybody in Abilene is happy to see you, but I'll be expecting you to keep your people in line while you're here."

Jeffries laughed, a short barking sound that contained little genuine humor. "Are you aware, Marshal," he asked, "that whenever there is trouble involving a circus, it is invariably the local citizens who cause the problem? I've been traveling with circuses all over Europe and America for the last twenty years, and I know what I'm talking about, sir."

"I'm sure you do," Travis agreed. "I don't doubt that you're right, either. All I'm asking is that you do your part. You see that your folks behave themselves, and I'll see to the people of Abilene. Deal?"

Jeffries studied him for a moment, then nodded abruptly. "As you say. Now, are there any local ordinances you'd particularly like to see enforced during our stay? Anything not designed to unfairly take money out of our pockets, that is?"

Travis grinned at the ringmaster. "You have run up against some crooked lawmen in your time, haven't you? Things aren't like that here, Professor, I can assure you. You just mind your business, and we won't have any trouble."

While Travis and Jeffries were talking, Cody's gaze wandered around the bustling camp. So far he had not spotted the buckskin-clad woman who had so captivated him during the parade, but a sudden outbreak of shots gave him a clue as to where she was.

Cody's hand jerked instinctively toward his gun as he heard the rattle of six-guns going off. Travis also tensed.

"Relax, both of you," Jeffries said easily as he noted their reactions. "That cacophony of gunshots is only our Miss Russell practicing."

"You're sure of that?" Travis asked.

"Quite sure. You're welcome to look for yourself, however."

Quickly, Cody said, "I'll check it out, Marshal."

"Go ahead," Travis told his deputy. "Just be careful. Don't get yourself shot."

"No chance of that," Cody said confidently. Hooking his thumbs in his belt, he strode toward the edge of the camp, toward the sound of the gunfire. Travis tried not to grin at the solemn expression on Cody's face and the serious tone in his voice. Just a lawman doing his duty, that was the impression Cody was trying to convey. The fact that the duty in question involved an attractive female had nothing to do with it, he seemed to be saying.

The shooting had slacked off somewhat as Cody neared its source, the blasts coming more slowly and deliberately now.

"Watch where you're going," a harsh voice called from his left, and he had to stop to allow one of the roustabouts to lead a camel past him. Cody frowned as the ugly animal gave him a wall-eyed stare.

Cody made his way through the crowd

and came to a large open area near the edge of the camp. The female trick shooter stood with a pair of pistols in her hands, her face a mask of concentration. She had pushed back her hat so that it hung on her shoulders by a thong around her neck, leaving her head uncovered. The midday sunshine struck red highlights in the thick chestnut hair.

As Cody watched, she slid the ivory-handled Colts back in their holsters, then nodded to a small man standing about thirty feet away. On second glance, Cody saw that he was not just small; he was, in fact, one of the midgets who had been dressed as a clown during the parade. Now he was wearing a plain white shirt and brown pants, and the greasepaint had been removed to reveal a broad, friendly face underneath a thatch of blond hair.

The man had several small wooden balls in his hand, and he threw them into the air one by one, scarcely pausing between each throw. Within instants, six of the balls were in the air.

Cody realized what the woman was going to attempt. The Colts seemed to leap into her hands as the balls hung in the air for a fraction of a second. The guns belched smoke and flame, each one blasting three times. Cody saw several balls explode into splinters.

He shook his head in amazement as only three of the balls thudded back onto the ground. She had hit three out of six. Considering the distance, the size of the targets, and their movement, that was remarkable.

The midget who was assisting her in her practice thought so, too. He hurried over to pick up the balls she had missed and called, "You got three of them, Dorinda! That's great!"

The woman shook her head. "That means I missed three, Andy. I can do better." She took fresh cartridges from the loops of the belt around her hips and began thumbing them into the cylinders of the Colts. "Set up the target."

The man called Andy walked to a nearby wagon and took out a folding wooden stand, much like an artist's easel. Instead of a canvas, it held a standard bull's-eye target. Andy set it up and then stepped back.

The woman holstered her guns, faced the target, and took a deep breath, squaring her shoulders. Then she palmed the right-hand Colt in an eye-blurring draw and fired three times, the shots coming so close together they sounded like one long roar. There was a split-second's pause as she tossed the gun effortlessly into her left hand and triggered it three more times.

Cody whistled softly as he saw four of the slugs smack into the bull's-eye. The other two missed being in the center only by a whisker.

The woman, hearing the whistle, glanced over and saw Cody standing there. She openly met his admiring gaze and asked, "What do you think?"

"Pretty good shooting," Cody said, smiling. He could not resist adding, "For a woman, that is."

"For a woman?" Andy exclaimed. "That's mighty good shooting for anybody!"

The woman regarded Cody coolly, her blue eyes taking in his dark good looks, the badge on his shirt, and the Colt riding on his own hip. A smile suddenly appeared on her face. "I saw you in town during the parade, Deputy," she said. "I didn't expect to see you again so soon."

"The marshal and I came out here on business," Cody explained, disarmed by a sudden lack of self-confidence. He was unaccustomed to women who did not bat their eyelashes at him and act coy. And he certainly was unused to talking to a woman who was wearing two Peacemakers.

"I'm Dorinda Russell," she said.

"Cody Fisher." He touched the brim of his hat. "Pleased to meet you, ma'am."

Dorinda inclined her head toward the target. "You said my shooting was pretty good—for a woman. Would you care to give it a try?"

Cody shifted his feet. "I'm not much of a trick shooter," he said. "I can't do a lot of fancy stuff."

"Surely you've shot at a target before."

"Well, sure—"

"Put up another target, Andy," Dorinda broke in, calling to the midget.

"You bet," Andy replied, a broad grin on his face. Cody muttered under his breath; he had not planned to demonstrate his own skill. As Andy tacked a fresh target onto the stand, he stepped up beside Dorinda Russell and slipped out his Colt to check the loads.

"Whenever you're ready, Mr. Fisher," Dorinda said lightly.

"Same trick?"

"Whatever you feel comfortable with."

Cody nodded and faced the target. As Dorinda had done, he took a deep breath, then drew his gun.

His draw was every bit as fast. He fired from the hip, three shots, then performed the same maneuver, switching hands and continuing the fire. He was a little slower at the shift, a little clumsier, and he fired only two shots afterward, since his gun had contained only five rounds.

Andy ran forward to check the target as Cody reloaded. The midget let out a yelp when he saw the five hits grouped closely within the bull's-eye. "All five in the center," Andy said shakily, as if he could not believe it.

Dorinda glanced sharply at Cody. "That's not bad either," she said slowly. "How are you at moving targets?"

"I've shot at a few," Cody replied simply.

She nodded, then called, "All right, Andy, you know what to do."

As Andy fetched more of the small wooden balls from the wagon, Cody slid another shell into his Colt, giving it the full complement of six this time. He said to the woman, "You've run into a lot of fellas who try to outshoot you."

"You're hardly the first," Dorinda replied wryly. "But you're good, I have to admit that."

"You're awfully good yourself," he said.

Andy returned from the wagon, three of the little balls in each hand. He took his position and asked, "You ready, mister?"

Cody nodded, his eyes never leaving the balls in the man's hands. Andy threw them into the air, one at a time as he had with Dorinda. Cody's gun was out by the time the first one had reached the apex of its flight, and the thunder of the six shots filled the air. Three of the thrown balls blew apart; the other three fell to the earth.

Andy laughed and seemed to be relieved that Cody had not bettered Dorinda on this test. He ran forward to pick up the unhit balls as Cody reloaded.

"That's very good," Dorinda said.

"I heard you say a few minutes ago that you could do better than three out of six."

She shrugged. "I have. One night I got five of them. That's the best I've ever done. The trick is more difficult than it looks."

Cody strolled over to Andy and asked, "Could I see those?"

Andy handed over the three balls. Cody looked at them for a moment, then nodded. He held one of them out to Dorinda, who had followed him over. "See that gouge on the side?" Cody asked. "One of my slugs did that. I just didn't hit it dead center."

113

Dorinda frowned dubiously, but she had to nod. "That's what it looks like, all right. Get the spinner, Andy." There was fresh determination in her voice.

Feeling eyes on him, Cody glanced over his shoulder to see that a growing crowd of circus people was watching him, their attention drawn by the unusual number of shots. He looked past the performers and roustabouts and saw Luke Travis and the professor approaching.

Andy came out of the wagon carrying a spoked wheel attached to a wooden stand. At the end of each spoke was a small circular attachment that held a ball of colored glass. Cody realized how the gadget worked. Andy would stand it up, set the wheel spinning, then get out of the way while Dorinda shot at the whirling glass balls.

Dorinda nodded to Andy, who carried the spinner a few more yards away. Professor Jeffries made his way through the crowd of onlookers, stepped up to Dorinda, and said, "My dear, I hope you realize that I do not intend to pay for everything you shoot to pieces in these impromptu contests."

"You know you can take it out of my salary, Professor," Dorinda returned sharply.

Jeffries sighed. "Very well. I suppose I should be getting accustomed to this by now."

Travis frowned at his deputy. "Seems like I recall somebody else acting like this, Cody, at Orion's recently," he said, referring to Ned Cahoon.

"Why don't you shoot first this time?" Dorinda said to her opponent.

Cody considered, then nodded. "Sure. Why not?" He looked at Andy, who was standing with a hand on one of the spinner's spokes. "Let 'er rip!"

Andy spun the wheel and scurried away to the side, while Cody's pistol seemed to leap into his hand. He emptied it, saw splinters of glass glinting in the air as some of the balls exploded, and then waited for the spinner to slow enough for the results of his shots to be visible.

Only two of the glass balls were shattered.

Cody frowned as Dorinda called, "Start it again, Andy!" The spinner had not yet come to a complete halt as Andy once more set it revolving at a dizzying speed. Dorinda drew and fired, blasting six bullets at the target.

"Stop it," she said to Andy as she holstered her gun.

He hurried forward and reached up to grasp one of the spokes, bringing the spinner to an abrupt stop. A cheer went up from the onlookers when they saw that all six of the remaining balls were gone.

Cody caught his breath. "Damn!" he said fervently.

Dorinda shook her head. "Actually, it's easier than it looks, once you're accustomed to it. I suppose it was unfair to make you go first." Her horse was tied to a stake nearby, and it had been grazing peacefully all through the exhibition, obviously unfazed by the sound of gunfire. Now Dorinda went over to him and pulled the Winchester from the saddle boot. She turned back to Cody and said, "How are you with a Yellowboy?"

"Never fired one," Cody admitted, admiring the recently developed model. "I'm pretty good with a Henry repeater, though."

Dorinda tossed the rifle to him. Cody caught it deftly, then turned it in his hands, studying with appreciation the intricate engraving on its breech and butt plates.

"Like to give it a try?" Dorinda asked.

Cody nodded.

Travis and Jeffries exchanged a glance and then turned away, leaving the others to watch the continuing show. As the two men strolled away from the clearing and back toward Jeffries's wagon, the ringmaster shook his head and said, "Ah, youth! To have some of that pride and exuberance again!"

"Cody's exuberant, all right," Travis agreed dryly. The Winchester began to crack behind them. "And he's got an eye for a pretty lady."

"A description which fits the fair Dorinda quite well," Jeffries commented. He changed the subject by adding, "Marshal, I was wondering if it would be possible to remain here in the vicinity of your town for several days?"

"I figured you'd just put on a show or two and then be back on the road as soon as possible," Travis said.

"That's the usual procedure, but I believe the troupe could use a rest. We've been traveling for quite a while now, and to be honest, we're all a bit tired. Besides, we seem to be experiencing a rash of problems with the wagons—axles breaking, wheels coming off, that sort of thing. I would like to check out all the vehicles and make any needed repairs while we're halted."

"Sounds reasonable enough." Travis nodded.

"And we could also put on some extra

performances while we're here. The troupe likes to try out new things, you know, while we have a live audience. You can't get an honest reaction from other circus folk. We've all seen too much to be properly amazed anymore."

Travis grinned. "Stay as long as you like, Professor, as long as there's no trouble."

"I assure you there won't be, Marshal." Jeffries sounded slightly distracted as he went on. "At least, I certainly hope not."

Back on the edge of the camp, amid clapping and cheering from the onlookers, Cody was admitting, "When it comes to trick shooting, a woman can do as well as a man."

"Sometimes better," Dorinda said with a smile.

Cody grinned at her. "Yeah. Sometimes better."

He had proved no match for her speed and accuracy with the Winchester. With handguns, they were on even terms, which in itself was amazing. He had never before encountered a woman who could shoot like Dorinda Russell. He was going to take this defeat gracefully, though, he told himself. The woman was too damned pretty to get mad at.

"Of course, there's a big difference between shooting at a target and shooting at some jasper who's shooting back at you," Cody could not resist pointing out. "That makes it just a bit harder to concentrate."

"I'm sure it does," Dorinda admitted. "And I'm glad I've never had to do that."

"I hope you never do." Cody hesitated. The crowd was drifting away, returning to their tasks now that the shooting display was over. Cody went on. "I think I'd better tell you about a fellow named Ned Cahoon."

Quickly, he explained about Cahoon and his drunken boasting. With a concerned look in her eyes, Dorinda asked, "Do you think he plans to interrupt the circus perfor-mance?"

"I wouldn't put it past him. He thinks he's the biggest curly wolf to ever come out of the woods. He might try to prove it."

Dorinda shrugged. "I wouldn't worry too much about him if I were you, Mr. Fisher. I've run into his type plenty of times since I joined the circus several years ago. I'm sure I can handle him."

Despite the confident words, Cody heard an undertone of doubt in her voice. "Well, I'll be around in case Cahoon does try some-thing," he said. "And why don't you call me Cody?"

She smiled warmly at him. "All right, Cody. And I'm Dorinda. Don't forget, our first performance is tonight."

"I'll be there," Cody promised with a grin.

VII

Orion McCarthy put all of his considerable strength into one final effort to overwhelm the danger facing him. As the muscles in his arm and shoulder bunched and rippled, he gave one last mighty heave. He groaned with the effort, as did the man sitting across the table from him.

The man gasped when the strain finally became too much for him. His knuckles rapped sharply against the tabletop as Orion forced his hand down.

The reaction from the crowd gathered around the table in Orion's Tavern was mixed. Most of the men cheered, because they had been backing Orion all the way. A groan of dismay went up from those few foolhardy souls who had bet on the big, rangy cowhand.

Orion stood up and clasped his hands over his head in a gesture of victory. Forcing a grin, he tried to conceal the aches and pains that coursed through his arm and shoulder.

His defeated opponent slumped back in his chair, rubbing his throbbing forearm. "I'll get you next time, Orion," he vowed. "You're gettin' old, you blamed Scotsman. You can't win forever."

"I'll give ye another chance, laddie." Orion laughed.

One of the other patrons slapped the tavern's proprietor on the back. "Nobody's ever beaten Orion at arm wrestling, and plenty have tried," he declared. "I'm willing to wager that nobody ever will."

"Ye'd best save ye money," Orion cautioned him. "Nobody wins forever. Sooner or later, somebody comes along who gets the better o' ye."

A shadow fell across the bright patch of sunlight that came in through the swinging batwing doors, a shadow large enough to blot out much of the light. Noticing it first, Orion turned to learn the cause.

A man stood just inside the saloon, his massive hands resting on the batwings he had shoved aside. Tall and broad, with a heavy jaw, dark bristling eyebrows, and not another hair on his head, the newcomer appeared quite intimidating until he abruptly smiled.

"Hello," he said in a mild voice as the knot of men around the table turned to stare at him. "Can a man get a drink in here?"

Orion nodded and broke away from the group of customers. "Aye, tha' he can. Welcome, stranger, to Orion's Tavern. Orion McCarthy is me name." He extended a hand toward the stranger.

The man took Orion's hand in a paw equally as large. "Bruno Wagner," he said. "Pleased to meet you, Mr. McCarthy."

One of the customers suddenly pointed a finger at Bruno Wagner. "Say, I recognize you now, mister. You're with the circus. You were in the parade."

"That's right," another man piped up. "You were wearing some kind of funny-lookin' mountain-lion pelt."

"Actually, it's a leopard-skin costume for my strong-man act," Wagner replied. He stepped into the tavern and crossed the room to the bar. Dressed in a plain shirt and pants, he was an impressive figure even without his circus costume. No one in the room was taller, and only Orion could match his width of shoulder. Busier than usual this afternoon, the tavern was crowded with people who had come to Abilene for the circus parade and were staying for the first performance that night. Following Orion's success in the arm wrestling match, most of the customers had gone back to their drinking. Many of them were watching the strong man, some surreptitiously, others openly staring.

Orion moved behind the bar and leaned his palms on it. "An' what'll ye be having, Mr. Wagner?"

"Call me Bruno, please. And I'll have cold beer."

"Me beer's as cold as ye'll find a'tween the Mississippi 'n' the Barb'ry Coast, Bruno," Orion boasted. He picked up a mug from the backbar and filled it, then slid the brew to a stop in front of Bruno.

The big bald-headed man lifted the mug to his lips, his throat working as he swallowed. When the beer was at least half gone, he thumped the mug back on the bar and smiled in satisfaction.

"It's good," Bruno said simply. "Not like back home in Munich, mind you, but good."

"Ah, 'tis a Prussian ye be."

Bruno finished off the beer and sighed. "Not for a long time. I've been in America for over twenty years. It's my home now. Or rather, wherever the circus goes is my home."

"Tha' circus o' yours has got folks in an uproar 'round here," Orion told him, leaning on the bar. " 'Tis the most exciting thing t'be hitting this town in a long time."

Bruno shoved the mug across the bar toward Orion and grinned. "I'm glad we can entertain people." He inclined his head toward the table where the arm wrestling contest had taken place. "Although it looked as if you were putting on quite a show when I got here."

Orion beamed as he refilled the mug and gave it back to Bruno. "Ye saw it, did ye?"

"Just the end of it. You were just polishing the fellow off when I got here, so I stayed outside on the boardwalk and watched through the door. I didn't want to distract you."

Orion waved a hand. " 'Twould'na mattered if ye had come in with trumpets blaring. I would'na noticed ye for concentration."

"Congratulations. I could tell you were quite an arm wrestler as soon as I saw you."

The tavern keeper's smile grew wide as he listened to the compliments from the burly but soft-spoken Wagner. A customer standing at the bar a few feet away from Bruno ventured, "Orion's taken on everybody in these parts and beaten 'em all. There's nobody better."

Bruno smiled at the man. "Is that so?"

"Orion's the undisputed champion of Abilene and the surrounding vicinity," the man went on. "Probably all of Kansas, too. If he hasn't wrestled all the young bucks yet, he will. Sooner or later they all come to Orion's seeking him out."

Bruno finished off the second mug of beer. "Well, good luck to you," he said to Orion. He began to dig in the pocket of his pants, searching for coins with which to pay for his drinks.

Orion's eyes narrowed thoughtfully, and he leaned forward. "Say," he said. "D'ye do any arm wrestling yeself, Bruno?"

Bruno touched his broad chest and shrugged his shoulders. "Me?" he asked. "Oh, I guess I've engaged in contests like that every now and then. My work at the circus doesn't leave me much time for such things, though."

A hush had fallen over the saloon as the customers waited to see what would happen. Orion clenched his fist and thumped it on the bar. "How about a match a'tween the two of us?" he suggested enthusiastically.

"Dinna be daft, man!" Old Bailey shrilled from his perch behind the bar.

Orion swung around sharply and shushed the bird. He told Bruno, "He dinna know what he's saying. He's just repeating what he's heard."

The strong man frowned. "I don't know," he said dubiously. "I'm not sure I'd be a match for you."

"Ah, 'twill all be in fun," Orion insisted. "We could even lay a small wager, if ye'd like."

"I'm not much of a betting man, but . . ." Bruno's voice trailed off as the customers began to crowd around him and urge him to accept Orion's challenge. Finally, the big man grinned and said, "Oh, what the hell? Why not?"

Orion reached across the bar and slapped him on the arm. "Tha' is the spirit!" He tried not to frown as he felt the iron hardness of the muscles under Bruno's shirt.

"What'll the stakes be?"

"How about drinks?" Orion suggested. "Ye win, 'n' 'twill all be on me for the rest o' the afternoon. I win, 'n' ye buy a couple o' rounds for the house."

Bruno nodded. "Fair enough."

As Orion came out from behind the bar and moved to the table where the previous match had taken place, an excited babble rose. The tavern's patrons quickly began to make bets among themselves. Orion overheard enough to know that most of the men were backing him, and his chest swelled with pride.

Orion grasped the back of a chair and moved it slightly before sitting down at the table. Opposite him, Bruno was arranging his chair to his liking. The customers formed a ring around the table, pressing closely together but staying back a little to give the two big men plenty of room.

From behind the bar, Old Bailey piped up once more, "Dinna be daft—"

"Shut up, ye feathered monstrosity!" Orion roared at the parrot, silencing him.

The wagering continued furiously among the spectators as Orion and Bruno each rested an elbow on the tabletop, moving their arms around to find the position they liked best. Orion flexed his blunt, thick fingers and rolled back the sleeve of his shirt to free his upper arm. Bruno pushed his own sleeve back so that it would not get in the way.

Finally, Orion asked, "Are ye ready?"

"Ready." Bruno nodded.

The two men leaned forward. Their hands met, thumbs locking as the fingers clasped. They steadied themselves, and Orion took a deep breath. "Somebody start us," he said.

One of the bystanders stepped up to the table. In a loud, clear voice, he said, "Ready . . . set . . . *go!*" He slapped the tabletop with his palm.

At first it was hard to tell that the match had begun. Save for a stiffening of the men's wrists and a sudden tautness that came over their features, there was no visible sign that Orion and Bruno were pitting their strength against each other.

Orion's eyes narrowed as he felt the power in Bruno's arm. After a moment his hand swayed perhaps a half-inch before he was able to counteract the pressure and apply some of his own. Slowly, their arms came back to the starting position and then moved a fraction in the other direction.

A bead of sweat popped out on Bruno's forehead as he bore down and moved Orion's hand back to the center of the table.

The tip of Orion's tongue came out and lightly touched his suddenly dry lips.

If either man was expecting an easy victory, it quickly became obvious that he would be disappointed. For long moments their arms remained motionless amid the excited hubbub of the spectators. Everyone in the tavern was gathered around the table, the ones in the back jockeying for better positions. At first there were murmurs of anticipation every time a combatant's hand moved slightly, but gradually the patrons came to realize that Orion and Bruno were only feeling each other out at this stage of the contest, trying to gauge each other's strength.

Soon a hushed silence fell over the big, low-ceilinged room. The breathing of Orion and Bruno became plainly audible, as were the occasional low-pitched grunts that escaped from each man. As they strained with effort, the match began to draw out over several minutes, minutes that undoubtedly seemed like hours to the two men seated at the table.

Orion remembered hearing that circus strong men could bend iron bars with their bare hands, lift horses, and perform other such feats of strength. He could well believe that Bruno Wagner was capable of that and more. There had been times over the years when Orion had wondered if he was going to succeed at defending his title as arm wrestling champion, but never before had he faced a test such as this.

He wondered fleetingly if Bruno's reluctance to engage in this contest had only been a ploy to draw him in. Maybe winning such matches was the way the man paid for his drinks in most towns. Orion tried to clear his mind and put those thoughts away. At this point it did not matter.

The muscles of each man's arm stood out in sharp relief from exertion as the contest passed the five-minute mark. Staring across the table, Orion saw that Bruno's face was bathed in sweat. The moisture trickling down his own face and dripping from his beard told Orion that he was in much the same shape.

Orion felt his strength ebbing. His match with the cowboy had taken place less than a half-hour earlier, while Bruno was probably fresh and rested. Orion's hand began to dip toward the table, and try as he might, he could not seem to halt the inexorable pressure.

When the back of his hand was only

inches from the tabletop, Orion finally brought the descent to a halt. The effort took every iota of strength he had remaining, or at least he thought it did. There was total silence as Orion held his position, and then from somewhere, some reserve deep inside him, he drew the strength to move Bruno's arm.

The strong man's eyes, already wide, seemed about to pop out of his head as he felt the fresh surge from Orion. Sensing that this would be his only opportunity, Orion poured on everything he had. Bruno's teeth gnashed together as he tried to hold back the Scotsman, to no avail.

Within a matter of moments Bruno's knuckles were the ones hovering just above the tabletop. Orion was at the peak of his effort, every sinew in his arm and shoulder and back throbbing with agony. All he needed was just another inch or two. . . .

His teeth dug into his lip, drawing blood as he realized he could not do it. Ever so slowly, Bruno was straightening his arm. The battle was almost over, and Orion knew it.

He held Bruno off for as long as he could, but once the tide had turned for the second time, it was less than a minute before Orion

131

felt his elbow bending back, his hand descending. The strength of the man from the circus was too much. Orion's hand abruptly thumped down on the table, prompting a cheer from the few men who had bet on Bruno.

Gasping for breath, the two men released each other. A grin spread over Bruno's face, and Orion could not help but return the smile. In a gesture that must have been painful, considering the strain his arm had just been under, Bruno extended his hand across the table.

Orion, not hesitating for an instant, firmly returned the handshake. Then wiping the sheet of sweat off his forehead, he said, "Congratulations, me boy. 'Twas one hell of a battle."

"Yes, it was," Bruno agreed. He winced as he moved his arm slightly, as if to make sure it was still working. "I think you deserve some congratulations, too, Orion. I've never run into anybody who gave me as much of a tussle as you. I really thought you had me for a minute."

"Aye, ye 'n' me both," Orion agreed. He glanced at his customers, many of whom were gloomily paying off on the bets they had just lost. Raising his booming voice,

Orion said, "This ain't a blasted undertakin' parlor. Ye gents drink up!"

"This round's on me!" Bruno called.

"Tha' was'na our deal," Orion protested. "I said I'd buy ye drinks for the rest o' the afternoon, laddie."

"If you can buy drinks for me, I can buy drinks for everybody else," the strong man said. "That's up to me, isn't it?"

Orion shrugged. "Aye, I reckon 'tis, a' tha'. But the least ye can do is come wi' me 'n' have a man's drink."

"What would that be?" Bruno asked with a laugh.

"Why, some genuine Scotch whisky, wha' else?"

Arm in arm, the two men went to the bar. Now that the arm wrestling match was over, the crowd seemed less interested in Bruno Wagner, although none of them turned down the drink he had offered to buy. Orion went behind the bar and, taking out his private bottle from under it, splashed some of the amber liquid into a fresh glass and handed it to Bruno. After pouring another drink for himself, Orion lifted his glass in a toast.

"To the man who ended me reign," Orion boomed. He tossed off the drink, then added, "O' course, when ye 'n' tha' circus move on, I'll be champion o' these parts again."

"I'll drink to that," Bruno declared, and he did just that.

Orion poured again, and although neither man realized it at that moment, another contest had begun. They kept drinking until the bottle was empty, and then Orion broke out another from his personal supply. The tavern began to quiet down again as the customers noticed what was happening.

Aside from a slight reddening of his face, Orion was showing no effects from the liquor. Neither was Bruno at first. As might be expected with a man of his size, he had quite a capacity. But as they continued drinking, the strong man's eyes began to glaze over. He swayed from side to side as he downed his latest drink.

Orion poured again.

A few moments—and a few drinks—later, Bruno lifted his glass, licked his lips in anticipation, sighed, and toppled like a huge tree. "Watch it there!" Orion yelled as a couple of men scurried to get out of Bruno's way.

Bruno hit the floor with a window-rattling thud. Orion leaned over the bar, peering down at him lying facedown in the sawdust, and asked anxiously, "Ye all right, lad?"

A resounding snore was the only answer from Bruno.

A smile of satisfaction raced across Orion's face before he could replace it with an expression of concern. Bruno might have won the arm wrestling match, but Orion had drunk him under the table.

"Somebody fetch a bucket o' water," Orion ordered the room at large, and one of the men hurried to comply. He went out through the batwings and came back a minute later with a bucket dipped from one of the watering troughs outside.

"Here you go, Orion," the man said as he handed the bucket over the bar. "What are you going to do with the water?"

"This fellow's ginna have t' perform in a show tonight, will'na he?" At a nod of agreement from the townsman, Orion went on. "Well, then, 'tis our duty t'wake him up, dinna ye know?"

He came around the end of the bar, stood over Bruno's sprawled figure, and hooked a booted foot under the shoulder of the passed-out strong man. With a grunt, Orion rolled him over. He grinned as he dashed the full contents of the bucket into Bruno's face.

135

Bruno came up off the floor with a spluttering yell, cursing in German. He subsided as the drunken nausea hit him.

"Dinna ye worry," Orion assured him. "We'll sober ye up, 'n' ye'll be back under the big top in no time. I'll just go make some coffee."

Bruno's moan followed him, and Orion grinned again.

At the same moment that Bruno Wagner and Orion McCarthy were testing their strength at Orion's Tavern, Dr. Aileen Bloom was next door in the small house that served as her medical office, where she was just finishing stitching up a long, deep cut in the leg of a man who had a farm near Abilene. He had suffered the injury when he had become careless with the scythe he was swinging, and Aileen had been required not only to tend to the wound but also to calm him down. The sight of so much blood had badly unnerved him, although the cut was more messy than it was serious.

"Thanks, Dr. Bloom," the man said sincerely, twisting his battered felt hat in his hands as he limped to the door. His overalls were stained with blood. He had been alone on the farm when the accident occurred and had driven himself into town in his buck-board. That in itself had been dangerous, since he could have passed out from loss of blood. "I'll pay you when I can, Doctor. I promise."

"Don't worry too much about that, Mr. Kettleman," Aileen told him as she followed him onto the porch of the little house. "Just take care of yourself and stay off that leg as much as you can for at least a week. I'm sure you'll pay me later."

"Yes, ma'am, I will." The farmer looked up as a man came galloping down Texas Street from the west. "That feller looks to be in a hurry."

"Indeed he does," Aileen agreed. She lifted a hand to shade her eyes from the afternoon sunlight as she tried to see if she recognized the rider. To her surprise, the man drew his mount to a halt in front of the office. He dropped down from the sad-dle and left the horse ground-hitched as he hurried up the walk toward the building.

Dressed in a soiled white shirt, a checked vest, dark corduroy pants, town shoes, and a bowler hat pushed back on his balding head, the disreputable-looking man was no cowhand or farmer, of that Aileen was cer-tain.

"I'm looking for the doc," he said as he came up to the porch. His accent immediately marked him as an easterner, and Aileen quickly concluded that he was one of the roustabouts from the circus.

"I'm Dr. Bloom," she answered quietly.

The man frowned. "A woman doctor?" he exclaimed. "Nobody told me nothing about that. Ain't there a real doctor in town?"

Aileen looked at him patiently. Her serenity concealed her irritation with such reactions.

Before she could answer, the farmer she had just treated spoke up. "Listen here," the man said sharply. "There ain't a better doctor, man or woman, in Kansas than Dr. Bloom here. And if you don't think so, I'll be glad to argue the point with you."

The stranger held up both hands, palms out in a gesture of peace. "Hold on, hold on," he said. "I didn't come here to get in a fight with some hayseed." He turned back to Aileen, ignoring the farmer's angry stare. "Look, Doc, I'm from Professor Jeffries's circus. We've got a hurt man out there, and the professor sent me to fetch a doctor. Can you go take a look at our guy?"

Aileen nodded. "Of course I'll go. What happened?"

"The count was working with his cats, and one of 'em got carried away. I didn't see von Benz, but I imagine he got mauled pretty good."

"Just let me get my bag." Aileen put her hand on the farmer's arm. "You go home and get some rest, Mr. Kettleman."

"Reckon you'll need any help out at that there circus?" Kettleman asked.

Aileen shook her head. "I'll be fine."

The roustabout shuffled his feet and said, "I don't want to hurry you, Doc, but I'm going to be in a lot of trouble if the count bleeds to death while I'm waiting for you."

"Yes. Just a moment." Aileen hurried into the house and returned a moment later carrying a bonnet and her black medical bag. She was pleased to see that the farmer had departed for home as she had requested. Gesturing at the buggy tied up in front of the building, she said to the roustabout, "Would you like to ride with me?"

"No thanks. I'll ride the horse and lead you to him."

Aileen tied the bonnet over her hair, placed her bag on the floorboard of the buggy, and climbed onto the seat after untying the horse's reins. The mare hitched to the buggy was strong and dependable, if not built for speed, with a sweet nature that Aileen liked. Aileen backed the buggy away from the boardwalk and turned it west down Texas Street. The roustabout fell in beside her on horseback.

In a few moments they were gazing across the prairie at their destination. The sight of the organized camp with the colorful big top dominating its center surprised and delighted Aileen. As she and the roustabout approached the circus camp, she considered the multitude of wonders awaiting the farmers, ranchers, and merchants of the area. Entertainment on wheels, pure and simple, that was what it was.

Driving past the makeshift corral with its grazing occupants, she spotted Travis and Cody riding toward her away from the heart of the camp. With a wave of his hand and a concerned look on his face, Travis motioned to her to stop.

"Is there some trouble, Aileen?" he asked as he drew up beside her buggy.

"Someone has been hurt here, Luke. Evidently one of the big cats attacked the trainer. I've come to see to his injuries."

"Marshal, we're in a hurry—" the roustabout began.

"Yes, just a moment," Travis said, frowning as he appraised Aileen's disheveled escort. Turning to Cody, Travis quickly instructed him to return to town. With a wave to Aileen, Cody spurred his horse and rode off. For a second time Travis looked sourly at the roustabout and then said firmly, "I'm coming with you."

A tiny smile lit Aileen's eyes as she flicked the reins. It was typical of this special man to show his concern for her. She enjoyed their relationship—the many evenings they shared dinner and good talk, the mutual respect they had for the way each worked. A rare, warm understanding had grown rapidly between them that had become very important to her.

The roustabout led them to four wagons grouped near the edge of the camp. Three of them were huge cages. Visible through the bars, lions and tigers were pacing restlessly. The fourth wagon was evidently the home of the big cats' trainer. It was enclosed, with a door on the rear and a set of removable steps leading down from the door. A man sat on those steps, but he stood as Aileen and Travis approached.

Aileen recognized the blond-haired man from the parade. He had exchanged his tight, gold-spangled costume for a white silk shirt with flowing sleeves and whipcord pants that were snug on his muscular legs. High black boots completed the outfit. One of the sleeves of the shirt had been cut away from his arm, and the crimson stain on the silk contrasted sharply with its whiteness.

The man stood calmly waiting for them as Travis dismounted and helped Aileen down from the buggy. Then he strode forward. Aileen had the medical bag in her left hand. The man reached out, caught hold of her right hand, and lifted it to his lips before she knew what he was doing. She stood there, flustered, as he said, "Count Lothar von Benz at your service, my dear."

Travis frowned but said nothing. When she recovered from her surprise and regained her voice, Aileen said, "I'm Dr. Aileen Bloom. The man who came to fetch me said you'd been injured, and I can see that he was right."

Count Lothar von Benz gestured casually at his bloodstained sleeve. "This scratch?" he said scornfully. "It is nothing! The professor, he simply likes to be careful."

Travis spoke up. "Where is the professor?" he asked.

"He went to see to other matters," von Benz replied. "There is a great deal to getting a circus ready for its first performance in a new town, Marshal. Although you would know nothing of that." The count turned his attention back to Aileen, his tanned face splitting in a smile. "I'm sorry you had to make the journey from town in this heat and dust over such a trifling matter, Doctor."

Aileen took a deep breath. The count was obviously used to overwhelming women with his easy charm. She did not intend for that to happen with her. "I'd better be the judge of how trifling it is, Count. Could I see your arm, please?" She kept her voice flat and matter-of-fact.

"Of course, dear lady." Von Benz pushed back the sleeve of his shirt to reveal a rough, bloody bandage around his arm. The smile on his face never budged as Aileen unwound the dressing to expose a long, jagged tear in the flesh of his inner forearm. The gash was a deep one, she could tell immediately.

"One of the lions did this?" she asked.

"My own fault, I assure you, not Fritz's. I was careless, and that is something one should never be when working with the big cats."

"Only big cats I ever ran up against were mountain lions and panthers," Travis said. "Always figured a good Winchester was the best way to handle them."

The count looked horrified. "Ah, Marshal, you do not understand. These animals are my babies! It is perfectly safe to be around them as long as everyone concerned never forgets who is in charge."

Aileen took hold of the count's arm, and his smile widened at the touch. "This is going to have to be cleaned and stitched up," she said. "I'm afraid it's going to hurt."

"Such pain is nothing," von Benz assured her. "It is but the price I pay for your delightful company, Doctor."

Travis turned away, muttering something under his breath.

Aileen opened her bag and placed it on the top step leading into the wagon. After removing a bottle of disinfectant, a needle, and a roll of surgical thread, she carefully poured a thin stream of the disinfectant over the wound. The count's eyes narrowed slightly, but other than that he showed no sign of the burning pain he had to be experiencing.

This cut was much like the one on the farmer's leg that Aileen had treated earlier, but the jagged edges of this wound made it more difficult to close. Aileen sat on the top step and had von Benz sit on the next one. She cradled his arm in her lap to work on it. The proximity made her very aware of the warmth of his body and a strange musky smell emanating from him. That came from being around the big cats so much, she supposed. But whatever the source, it was compelling.

She tried to concentrate on her work and ignore what she was feeling. The count was undeniably attractive, but that was no reason she should react like some silly schoolgirl.

As she worked, von Benz kept up the conversation, telling her several anecdotes about his work with the lions and tigers. He was probably trying to keep his mind off the pain, she reasoned, as well as attempting to charm her.

Aileen lifted a hand to brush back a strand of brunette hair that had fallen across her forehead, but before she could do it, the count reached across his body with his other hand and ever so gently tucked back the hair. Aileen felt warmth suffusing her face.

Dammit, she was blushing! She glanced up to see Travis watching—glaring—from several yards away. Obviously, he was disturbed by what he was seeing.

Was he bothered because he did not trust the count, Aileen wondered, or could it be that he was . . . jealous?

Aileen smiled to herself, pleased, although Travis had no right to be jealous. There was nothing more between them than friendship and respect. Maybe someday, when the shadow of Travis's late wife had completely faded away . . .

And there was certainly nothing between her and this smooth-talking European. They had just met, and his sort of charm did not appeal to an intelligent, educated woman such as herself.

She finished stitching the wound, nodding in satisfaction as she studied the results of her work. There would be a scar—there was no avoiding that with such a deep cut—but it should not be too bad, she thought. Replacing the needle and thread in the bag, Aileen took out a roll of cloth, wrapped it around the wound, and tied it in place.

"There," she said. "That should just about do it."

The count flexed his arm, nodding in

approval. "A superb job, just as I expected," he pronounced. "You have my sincerest appreciation, Doctor. How much do I owe you, my dear?"

Cringing inwardly, Aileen wished he would not call her his dear. "Two dollars ought to cover it," she said.

Von Benz nodded. "I shall have the professor pay you before we leave Abilene."

Travis, who was standing close enough to hear the conversation, frowned and said, "Folks usually pay the doctor after she helps them." He ignored the shake of Aileen's head that she gave him.

"I assure you, Marshal, the good doctor shall be paid. It is just that I seldom carry money on my person. Besides, the professor customarily takes care of such circus-related expenses."

"It's all right," Aileen said quickly. "I'm not worried about getting paid. Money was never the reason I went into medicine."

"Ah, of course not," the count agreed. "You simply wished to help people, correct?"

"Something like that." Aileen felt vaguely embarrassed by his words.

"Perhaps in addition to the fee, you would care to join me for a late supper tonight after the performance," von Benz said smoothly. "I feel that it is the least I can do to repay your kindness."

Aileen smiled and shook her head, aware that Travis was watching her reaction. "I'm sorry, Count," she said. "That sounds lovely, but I'm afraid I'm accustomed to retiring early. A doctor never gets enough sleep, you know."

"But of course." The count took the refusal in stride. Again he took her hand and lifted it to his lips. "As I said, you have my deepest thanks."

Aileen smiled, undeniably flattered by his advances. She knew quite well, though, that in a few days Count Lothar von Benz would be moving on with the rest of the circus, and she had no desire to get involved in a temporary relationship. She was the type of woman whose goals had always been more permanent, romantically and otherwise.

Travis fell in beside her as she started back to the buggy, carrying her medical bag. Without looking at her, the marshal commented, "A man like that count can really set a woman's heart a-flutter."

Aileen glanced over her shoulder and saw von Benz lift his arm in a farewell salute. "I suppose," she said as she returned the wave.

"He is rather handsome, if you like that type."

Travis said nothing, not wanting to give her further opportunity to talk about how attractive the count was.

They had just reached Aileen's buggy when Professor Jericho Jeffries and another man came hurrying up. "Hold on there, Marshal!" Jeffries called. "There's been a spot of trouble."

"If you're talking about that Count von Benz," Travis said, "Dr. Bloom here has already tended to him."

Jeffries shook his head. He looked agitated, and the man with him appeared ready to burst into tears. Before Jeffries could say anything else, the young man exclaimed, "He's dead!"

"Dead?" Travis snapped, a frown on his face. "Who's dead?" The young man's voice was familiar, but Travis could not place him.

"My horse," the man said raggedly. "I went into the tent to get him ready for the show, and I found him then. He'd been shot!"

"Eliot fetched me immediately," Jeffries added. "I thought you might have met the doctor and stayed, so we came to look for you."

Travis studied the young man called Eliot, then said as he recognized him, "You're that clown who was in the parade this morning, the one with the horse that nearly stomped Thurman Simpson."

"Simpson!" Eliot spat. "He's the one who did it, Marshal. He said my horse ought to be shot, so he came out here and did it!"

Travis took a deep breath. "Let's not accuse anyone just yet, son. I know you're upset, but why do you think Simpson might have killed your horse?"

Eliot reached into the pocket of his pants and pulled out a small pistol. Travis recognized it as an Allen and Thurber .34 Pepperbox. Eliot thrust it at him, butt first, and said, "I found this in the straw just inside the tent."

Travis took the pistol and sniffed its fat barrel. "Been fired recently, all right," he said.

"Look at the butt," Jeffries told him.

Travis turned the weapon in his hands, his frown deepening as he saw the name engraved on one of the wooden grips: T. Simpson.

Standing close beside him, Aileen saw the name, too, and said, "Why, I can't believe that Mr. Simpson would kill anything. He's a schoolteacher."

"That doesn't mean he can't pull a trigger," Travis replied grimly. He broke open the cylinder of the Allen and Thurber and saw that one bullet had been fired from it. "We'd better take a look at the horse."

An examination of the slain animal revealed a small-caliber bullet wound in its head, and Travis had to agree that the little pocket pistol was probably the weapon that had been used. "You heard him this morning," Eliot said, grief and anger mingled in his voice. "He said the horse ought to be shot. Well, he did it, and he must have dropped that gun while he was running out of here."

Moved by the young man's emotional state, Aileen reached out and took his hand to comfort him. Travis nodded thoughtfully. "How long had it been since you saw the horse alive?" he asked.

"A couple of hours at least, maybe a little longer," Eliot answered.

"Whoever did the shooting could have done it while that female sharpshooter was practicing," Travis suggested. "My deputy burned quite a bit of powder during that session, too, and most of the people in camp were watching." Travis rubbed his jaw. "More than likely, that's when it happened."

"What are you going to do about this, Marshal?" Jeffries demanded.

Travis glanced through the tent's entrance at the lowering sun. "You have a performance to put on in a little bit. How about if we wait until after it's over to question Simpson?"

"You're going to arrest him, aren't you?" Eliot asked.

"I'm going to talk to him," Travis said. "Don't worry, son, I want to get to the bottom of this just as much as you do."

"Very well," Jeffries agreed after a moment's thought. "After the performance, then. And I want to be there to represent the interests of Eliot here."

Travis nodded. "That's fine. I'll see you at the office later tonight."

"I'll be there."

Travis and Aileen walked slowly back to her buggy. "Do you really think Thurman Simpson would shoot a horse like that?" Aileen asked.

"I don't know what he's capable of, to tell you the truth," Travis admitted. "But I'm going to find out. I don't want this blowing up into an even bigger problem."

Aileen nodded, hearing the grim note in his voice. He was worried about his town. Maybe with good reason.

VIII

The first performance of the circus that night was a dazzling spectacle that Cody would never forget. Standing on the sawdust-covered ground inside the big tent, he and Travis had positioned themselves just behind a waist-high wooden fence that encircled the large central ring. Around the inside of the tent, tiers of benches providing seating for the audience had been erected during the afternoon. Tonight nearly every space was full. What seemed like half the town had come to witness Professor Jericho Jeffries's Traveling Circus and Extravaganza.

A trumpet volley announced the beginning of the performance. Accompanied by stirring marching music played by the band, the members of the troupe paraded into the big top through a large side opening. They marched into the huge central ring and circled it, waving and smiling at the audience. Their colorful costumes glittered in the bright torchlight that illuminated the interior of the tent. Horses and elephants wore spangled headdresses topped with fluttering ostrich plumes, and the animals pranced and trumpeted in response to the cheers and gasps from the crowd.

An excited thrill ran up Cody's spine, and a tap on his shoulder startled him. He turned to Travis. "You head that way," Travis told his deputy, gesturing. "I'll go the other, and we'll meet on the far side. Keep your eyes open for Ned Cahoon."

"You think he'll try to make trouble tonight, Marshal?" Cody asked.

"I don't know," Travis answered honestly. "He hasn't been seen in town since Orion threw him out of his saloon last night, but there's no telling what a young hothead like Cahoon will do. He bragged so much about causing trouble for the circus that he may feel he has to go through with it."

Cody nodded. "If I spot him, I'll see that he doesn't bother anybody."

Travis reached out and caught Cody's arm as the deputy started to turn away. "Be careful," he cautioned. "Cahoon's not as good as he thinks he is, but he could still be dangerous."

Cody grinned cockily. "Hell, Marshal,

you know he can't hold a candle to either one of us."

"Just watch yourself anyway."

Cody was probably right, Travis mused as he strolled away, but the only way to prove it was to trade shots. Travis wanted to avoid that if possible.

Professor Jericho Jeffries strode to the center of the big ring, wearing his scarlet coat and shiny top hat. He carried a canvas megaphone in one hand and waved it, acknowledging the thundering applause from the audience. When he reached the center of the ring, he lifted the instrument to his lips.

"Laaadies and gentlemen!" he bellowed. "Preeesenting the most amazing, most astounding, biggest show this side of the great Atlantic Ocean . . . Professor Jericho Jeffries's Traveling Circus and Extravaganza!"

The tent erupted in another thunderous avalanche of applause and cheers.

Travis paused, resting his hands on the fence around the ring. He had to admire Jeffries's showmanship. Alone in the center of the ring, he cut a dramatic figure.

Looking across the ring, Travis noted that Cody had stopped to watch as well, unable to resist the lure of the ringmaster's voice. Travis grinned. He could not very well say anything to the young man about it when he was doing the same thing.

As the clapping and whistling died down, Jeffries continued. "Ladies and gentlemen, I direct your attention to those paragons of equestrian agility, those magicians on horseback—the incredible Carstairs family!"

As the eyes of the audience followed Jeffries's outflung hand, the three trick riders galloped into the arena through the big main entrance. They rode three magnificent white stallions, the two men flanking the woman, and as the enthusiastic spectators watched, each of them in turn dropped from the tiny saddles, seemed to bounce off the ground, and then reappeared on horseback.

The act continued for several minutes. One of the men rode two horses roman-style, standing up with one foot on each horse. The woman balanced on her head in the saddle, then somersaulted off the animal into the saddle of another horse in mid-gallop. Travis admired the horsemanship of the performers as they attempted things that even a Plains Indian might not dare.

When the trick riders had dazzled the audience, they rode out of the tent the same way they had entered, and on the way out they nearly trampled one of the clowns. The man in baggy pants was wandering into the ring, seemingly paying no attention to where he was going. Travis caught his breath as the clown had to leap frantically out of the way of one of the horses, but then as the man rolled over and came up scratching his head quizzically, the marshal realized that the close call was all part of the act. Laughter erupted from the audience as they saw the puzzled look on the clown's painted face.

Travis continued his journey around the big top as several more clowns joined the first one for some controlled chaos. There was no sign of Ned Cahoon among the crowd, at least as far as Travis could see. In this crowd, however, it would be easy to overlook the would-be troublemaker.

"Now, ladies and gentlemen," Jeffries announced when the clowns had tumbled out of the ring, "I have the great pleasure to introduce to you one of the bravest men I have ever known. Only this afternoon, he suffered a grievous injury in the course of his preparations to thrill you tonight. However, he insisted that he carry on with his performance as planned. Good people of

Abilene, I give you Count Lothar von Benz . . . and his pets!"

Through the entrance came the three barred wagons bearing the big cats. They were being driven by roustabouts armed with rifles for the protection of the audience should the big cats become unruly. The count himself stood atop the lead wagon, splendid in his costume with a bandage on his arm, a coiled whip in his hand, and a revolver strapped to his side. As the wagons came to a stop, von Benz hopped lithely to the sawdust and bowed to the crowd. The roustabouts climbed on top of the wagons and got ready to lift the doors on the rear of the vehicles. Several clowns came running into the ring carrying chairs and small platforms, which they placed in a seemingly haphazard arrangement near the count.

When von Benz gestured to the roustabouts, they opened the wagons, and the lions and tigers came bounding out to the gasps of the crowd. A big smile on his face, the count turned to face the animals and barked commands to them in a language Travis did not understand. Von Benz cracked his whip, although the marshal noticed that he kept the tip away from the cats themselves. Evidently they were trained to respond to just the sound of the whip.

Travis watched as von Benz put the big cats through their paces under the watchful eyes of the armed roustabouts. The sleek animals leaped from one pedestal to another at the count's commands, performing tricks almost as a dog would have. As fascinating as it was, Travis instinctively disliked the count, so he turned to scan the crowd.

The first person he noticed there did not make him feel any better about von Benz. Aileen Bloom was sitting halfway up the tiers of benches, watching the count's performance with rapt attention. Aileen probably just wanted to make sure her medical treatment was satisfactory and that the count was not having any trouble using the injured arm. Not that it was any of his damned business, Travis muttered to himself.

Sitting next to Aileen was Sister Laurel. At the other end of the bench was Agnes Hirsch, and the space between was filled with the orphans in Sister Laurel's care. The faces of the children were covered with huge smiles, and Travis thought he had never seen such a happy-looking bunch. Directly behind them sat the Reverend Judah Fisher and Orion McCarthy, an unlikely duo but one that would have no trouble keeping order if the children became too rambunctious.

He strolled around the ring, and a few minutes later, met Cody coming toward him. "Any sign of Cahoon?" Travis asked the deputy.

Cody shook his head. "Nope. No trouble at all, in fact. Everybody seems to be too interested in watching the circus to raise a ruckus."

"Good. Let's hope it stays that way." Travis grinned. "We might as well sit down and watch the show ourselves."

"Sounds good to me."

Some of the townspeople on the front row were happy to move over and make room when they saw the two lawmen searching for a place to sit. Travis and Cody settled down on the wooden bench, content for the moment to be spectators. Both of them stayed alert for anything unusual, however.

After a while, the acts began to run together in Travis's mind. He laughed at the clowns who performed between each of the major attractions, was properly impressed by the strong man—who, to Travis's trained eye, looked a little hung over—and applauded with the rest of the crowd as two men juggled razor-sharp knives.

Although Cody was interested in the other acts, he was clearly impatient for Dorinda Russell to make her appearance. Finally Professor Jeffries went to the center of the ring and said through his megaphone, "And now for a special treat, ladies and gentlemen, we have a young woman who is not only lovely . . . she is also the most deadly shot with any sort of weapon that you will ever see! Yes, my friends, I am speaking of that belle of the plains, that eagle-eyed sharpshooting beauty . . . Miss Dorinda Russell!"

Enthusiastically, Cody clapped, then put his fingers in his mouth and whistled shrilly as Dorinda came riding into the ring on a handsome palomino stallion. The horse reared, pawing the air, and then Dorinda urged him into a gallop. As she raced through the course, which had been set up after the previous act, she slipped her Colts from their holsters and fired from horseback, shooting at targets on the stakes that marked her course. While she was entertaining the crowd, several roustabouts worked ropes that were attached to the peak of the tent, opening the canvas and rolling it back like a curtain, so that the entire center overhead was exposed to the sky. This was to ensure that when she fired at targets hurled into the air, the bullets did not tear the tent to shreds.

Like nearly everyone else in the tent, Cody was fascinated by the lovely young woman and could not tear his eyes away from her. Travis, on the other hand, was turning in his seat to glance toward the main entrance of the tent. If Ned Cahoon was going to show up, this would be the time for him to cause trouble.

A sudden flurry of motion near the entrance brought Travis to his feet, but he was too late. A tall figure in flashy range clothes burst into view. One of the roustabouts lunged toward Ned Cahoon as the man strode toward the ring. Cahoon met him with a solid punch to the jaw, and the roustabout went sprawling. More of the circus laborers started to close in, and a pistol appeared in Cahoon's fist.

Travis dug a sharp elbow into Cody's side, jerking his attention away from Dorinda. "It's Cahoon!" Travis barked. "Let's go!"

Cody cursed as he spotted Cahoon, and then both lawmen lunged from their seats and vaulted the rail around the ring.

Cahoon was threatening the roustabouts with his pistol, and they had no choice but to fall back and let him pass as he strode into the ring.

Dorinda had not noticed the potential trouble. She had dismounted and started on another portion of her act with the help of the midget called Andy, who was made up as a clown. Andy had several dinner plates in his hand, and at Dorinda's signal, he began to toss them into the air, much as he had done with the wooden balls during the afternoon practice session. Dorinda had holstered her guns, and now she drew with blinding speed, shattering the plates with her shots.

The final plate left Andy's hand and spun high into the air, but before Dorinda could fire at it, a shot rang out from behind her. She jumped, startled, as the plate exploded into a thousand pieces.

Dorinda turned to see Ned Cahoon swaggering toward her, smoke curling from the barrel of his revolver. Behind him, Luke Travis and Cody Fisher were hurrying forward, guns drawn. Although Dorinda had never seen Cahoon before, she knew from what Cody had said that this stranger had to be him.

"Howdy, little lady," Cahoon said as he came to a halt several yards away. "Sorry if I scared you there. I just thought you might like to see how a real man shoots."

By now the audience realized that something was wrong, and a tense silence was dropping over the tent. Cahoon's words were clearly audible to Travis and Cody as they approached.

Dorinda faced him calmly and said, "You're disrupting my performance. I'd appreciate it if you'd go back and sit down and watch the show."

Cahoon grinned arrogantly. "You would, would you? Well, I can't do that, lady. You see, my name's Ned Cahoon, and I aim to prove that there's no way any woman can outshoot me."

"Come now, Mr. Cahoon," Dorinda replied. "I'm sure you don't really need to prove that."

From behind Cahoon, Cody said, "He sure as hell doesn't."

"Drop the gun, Cahoon," Travis added. He and Cody stood with their weapons leveled at the young gunman.

Cahoon did not turn around. Still grinning, he said, "So, the law dogs are here, eh?"

Cody's face was dark with anger. When Cahoon made no move to put down his pistol, Cody said, "If you really want a shooting match, Cahoon, just turn around, and I'll be glad to oblige."

Before Cahoon could reply, Dorinda stepped closer and shook her head. "Thank you, Marshal," she said past Cahoon. "You, too, Cody. But I'd be obliged if you'd let me handle this."

"What?" Cody exclaimed. "But this fellow—"

"Wants a shooting match, as you said," Dorinda replied. "I don't mind testing my skills against his."

Twisting his head to smirk over his shoulder, Cahoon said, "That's what the little lady wants, Marshal. You ain't goin' to disappoint her, are you?"

Travis looked closely at Dorinda and saw the confidence in her eyes. With a nod, he holstered his gun and said, "Miss Russell wants to handle this, Cody. I think we should give her a chance to do just that."

"Thank you, Marshal." Dorinda nodded.

Cody began to protest, then stopped as Travis motioned him to step away. Keeping his gun drawn, Cody joined Travis, although he kept glancing over his shoulder at Dorinda and Cahoon.

"What the hell are we doing, Marshal?" Cody demanded in rasping whisper. "You know Cahoon can't be trusted!"

"I know," Travis agreed. "That's why we're going to stay close by. But I saw Miss Russell shoot against you this afternoon. I think Cahoon is in for a rude surprise."

Dorinda turned to Andy, who was standing nearby with a concerned expression on his painted face. "Fetch the silver dollars," she told him gently.

Andy grinned and nodded, then hurried over to Dorinda's horse. Stretching up on tiptoes, he reached into the saddlebags.

"Plates are too easy," Dorinda told Cahoon in a cool voice. "Let's make it more of a challenge, shall we?"

Cahoon still had the cocky grin on his face. "Whatever you say, lady. All I know is, the woman ain't been born who can outshoot me."

"We'll see," Dorinda said.

Travis saw Professor Jericho Jeffries hurrying into the ring. He met the ringmaster and stopped him by laying a hand on Jeffries's arm. "Hold on," Travis said. "Miss Russell's got everything under control."

"But . . . but that ruffian is interrupting her act!" Jeffries sputtered. "He attacked one of my men!"

"I saw that." Travis nodded. Glancing toward the tent's entrance, he saw Cahoon's two friends there, surrounded by angry roustabouts. The two men were making no threatening moves and were watching Cahoon to see if he could make good on his boast. Travis said to Jeffries, "You'd better make sure your men don't jump Cahoon's friends. I don't want a brawl here."

Staring angrily at Travis for a few seconds, Jeffries then nodded. "All right," he said, turning to leave. Under his breath, he muttered, "Trouble, always trouble—"

Andy, ready with the handful of silver dollars, asked, "Who's going first?"

Dorinda glanced at Cahoon, who said, "Hell, go ahead. Ladies first, I reckon. Ain't gonna matter, anyway."

Dorinda nodded. "All right, Andy. One at a time."

The little clown took one of the silver dollars and flung it high into the air. Dorinda drew smoothly and fired a split second later, seeming not to aim at all. The coin went spinning wildly to one side. Andy ran to retrieve it, and when he bent to pick it up, he grinned broadly and waved the silver dollar over his head. The crowd could see the bullet hole punched through its center.

Cahoon snorted. "Not bad," he said grudgingly. To Andy, he called, "Hey, little feller! Toss two of 'em up this time."

Andy looked to Dorinda for instructions. She nodded, so Andy took two of the coins in his hand, drew back his arm, and threw them straight up in the air.

Cahoon still had his gun in his hand. He snapped it up, extending his arm, and triggered twice. The look of concentration on his face fell away and became a triumphant grin as he saw both dollars knocked crazily from their course. With a frown, Andy went to pick them up. He glanced at Dorinda again, and once more she nodded. Andy raised the coins so the audience could see that both of Cahoon's slugs had found their mark.

Slowly, Dorinda took a fresh cartridge from her shell belt and replaced the spent one in her gun. "Six, Andy," she said quietly.

"Dorinda!" the midget yelped.

Cody looked at Travis, eyes wide. "Shoot, nobody could hit six at a time like that!" he exclaimed.

Cahoon was trying not to look impressed. "Easy to say, lady," he sneered. "Not so easy to do. You sure you even want to try it?"

Dorinda did not bother to answer. She turned to Andy with a slight smile tugging at her mouth and said, "Are you ready?"

Andy swallowed. Holding a stack of six silver dollars in his right hand, he nodded jerkily. "If you're sure, Dorinda."

She settled the Colt in its holster, the smile still on her face. "Now!" she snapped.

Andy threw the coins, and the gun appeared in Dorinda's hand as if by magic. Six blasts rang out as she dropped smoothly to one knee. The silver dollars spun wildly, all of them dropping to the sawdust far apart from each other. Andy jerked his head from side to side, trying to locate them all. He started running from coin to coin, raising each one into plain sight as he found it. The grin on his face got wider and wider.

"Damn," Cody breathed in awe.

The silence in the tent deepened with the discovery of each coin. One by one, Andy showed off the dollars, each of them cleanly pierced by a slug. When he lifted the sixth and final coin from the sawdust and the audience saw the hole in it, a thunderous wave of applause and cheering burst out, washing over the arena and the woman standing coolly in its center.

Ned Cahoon's face was red with rage. He stared at Dorinda in angry disbelief, and his fingers whitened as his grip on the pistol tightened.

"I wouldn't even try if I were you, Mr. Cahoon," she told him. "That would only make you appear more foolish."

Cahoon spun to face Andy. "You got more of them coins?" he demanded of the midget.

"You bet," Andy replied. "Six more, in fact."

"Then throw 'em, you goddamn dwarf!"

Andy's features tightened in anger. "Sure," he said. "Glad to oblige, big man."

Cody looked sideways at Travis. "Marshal . . . ?"

"Let him try," Travis said. "That's what he wants."

When Cahoon nodded his readiness, Andy threw the silver dollars into the air. Cahoon drew and fired, triggering just as fast as Dorinda had done, but everyone in the tent knew right away that he had hit only two of the coins. The others fell straight to the sawdust, untouched.

Again there was applause, obviously for

Dorinda. As the cheers of the crowd fell on his ears, Cahoon's rage built. He stalked toward Dorinda, the empty gun still in his hand.

"You bitch!" he snarled. "Try to make a fool out of me, will you!"

"I'd say you did that yourself, Mr. Cahoon," she replied quietly. Behind Cahoon, Travis and Cody were closing in.

"That was just trick shootin'!" Cahoon ranted. "It don't mean a damn thing! Why don't you put some bullets back in that gun and we'll see who's really better? Just you and me, bitch!"

Dorinda's features were still calm, but she had gone pale under his abuse. "Maybe that's what we should do," she snapped.

Travis stepped up behind Cahoon, thumbing back the hammer of his Colt. "No," he said flatly. "There won't be any gunfighting in here. Too many innocent people could get hurt."

His voice shaking, Cahoon said, "We ain't in Abilene now, Travis. You got no say in this!"

Cody spoke up. "Then I'll take off my badge, and you and I will go outside to settle things, Cahoon. How about that?"

Cahoon, his eyes glittering madly, stared

at the deputy. "That's twice you've called me out, Fisher," he grated. "You and me, we'll settle things, all right, but not now. Not with Mr. High-and-Goddamn-Mighty Marshal here ready to butt in."

Travis drew a deep breath. "All right, Cahoon," he said. "Get the hell out of here." He glanced over and saw that Jeffries had come up to Dorinda to make sure she was all right. "That is, if the professor here doesn't want to press charges against you for disrupting his show."

Jeffries shook his head. "I just want the man out of here, Marshal."

"You heard him, Cahoon," Cody said. "Out!"

Humiliated at every turn, Cahoon jammed his empty gun back in its holster. "I'm goin'," he said. "But I won't forget this."

He stalked out of the arena, past the roustabouts at the entrance. His two companions fell in beside him, and the three of them vanished into the shadows outside the tent.

Cody holstered his gun and went over to Dorinda. "Are you all right?" he asked anxiously.

"I'm fine," she replied with a smile.

"Cahoon's not the first one to pull something like this. Just the worst, maybe."

"Do you think he'll be back, Marshal?" Jeffries asked.

"I reckon there's a good chance he will be," Travis said wearily. "But we'll deal with that when the time comes. Right now, Professor, I'd say you've got the rest of a show to put on before that audience gets restless."

"Yes, indeed," Jeffries said with a humorless laugh. "The show, as they say, must go on."

The evening's performance continued smoothly, and the interruption by Ned Cahoon was soon forgotten as the audience was carried away by the glamor and spectacle of the circus.

Travis was fascinated by the acrobats as they performed on the high wire and the trapeze. He had never been particularly afraid of heights, but a shiver went through him as he watched the aerialists spinning through midair in their bright costumes. At least there were nets underneath to catch them in the event of an accident. It was a shame, Travis thought, that it had taken the falls by Gil Palmer and Jeffries's own wife before that reasonable precaution was taken.

Finally the performance came to an end with Professor Jeffries thanking the crowd and inviting them to return the next evening for more thrills and excitement. "All of our performers will have new tricks to amaze you," he promised. "Now, good night, everyone!"

The crowd began filing out of the tent through the big main entrance and several smaller openings. The group of children from the orphanage were still wide-eyed and chattering and would not calm down enough to sleep for at least a week. Sister Laurel, the Reverend Judah Fisher, and Agnes Hirsch tried to keep them moving in an orderly fashion, but it was not easy. The sideshow attractions were still open outside, and the bright lights drew the interest of the children.

In addition, many of the animals were being taken back to their cages for the night. Michael Hirsch's eyes grew larger as he saw a couple of elephants being led away.

Michael cast a quick glance toward his sister, Agnes, who was busy keeping an eye on the other children. So was Sister Laurel. Judah Fisher had stopped to speak briefly to his brother as Cody and Travis also left the tent.

This was his chance, and Michael realized it. He was willing to risk getting in trouble to see the mighty elephants up close. He hung back from the others for a moment, and as soon as the gap increased enough, he darted away, ducking between two parked wagons.

He had taken three steps in the shadows when he ran into someone. Bouncing back, Michael lost his balance and sat down hard on the ground. He shook his head and looked up, expecting to get into trouble for plowing into an adult. Instead, he found himself looking at what he took at first glance to be another youngster. "Sorry, kid," Michael said, climbing to his feet and brushing himself off.

"Hold on there," the other person said, and it was no child's voice that issued from his throat. "Where are you going in such a hurry, son?"

Michael stared, peering intently in the gloom at his companion. He said in shocked recognition, "You're that clown! The one with the lady sharpshooter!"

Andy grinned. "That's right. I'm a joey.

That's what us clowns call ourselves, you know."

"What happened to your face?" Michael asked. "You look like . . . I don't know, a . . ."

"A normal person?" Andy asked, still smiling. "Yeah, once the paint is washed off, most of us are. Of course, some of us are a little shorter than others. Say, you didn't tell me why you were in such a hurry."

"I was going to see the elephants," Michael said. "I never saw elephants before tonight."

"Fond of the mighty pachyderms, eh? What's your name, kid?"

"Michael. Michael Hirsch."

"Well, Michael," Andy said, "you may not know this, but the elephant handlers always hire some of the local fellows to haul water for them. Those big beasts drink a lot, let me tell you. Come on with me, and I'll see if we can get one of those jobs for you."

"You mean it?" Michael asked incredulously. That would be the height of good fortune, to have a job that would actually pay him to be around the circus animals.

"Well, I can't promise anything, but I tell you what. Touch me on the head."

Michael frowned. "What?"

Andy patted the top of his head. "Touch me on the head. It's good luck to touch a clown, and it's especially good luck to touch a midget clown. That's an old circus superstition, and it can't hurt anything."

"Well . . . all right." Feeling rather foolish, Michael reached out and patted Andy on the head.

"Now, come on. By the way, do your parents know where you are?" Andy asked.

Michael shook his head. "I don't have any parents. I'm an orphan."

Andy grimaced. "Sorry, Michael. My folks died when I was pretty young, so I know how you feel. I'm just glad I found the circus. Traveling with it is like having a great big family, and they're good people. Have you ever given circus life any thought?"

Michael swallowed as he followed the clown. "I—I hadn't," he admitted, "until now."

But he would in the future, Michael knew. He would give the matter a great deal of thought.

Luke Travis was at his desk in the marshal's office an hour later when a knock came on the door. Travis pushed his paperwork aside and got up to answer the summons. Not surprisingly, Professor Jericho Jeffries stood on the boardwalk outside.

"Good evening, Marshal," Jeffries said as Travis stepped back to let him into the office. The ringmaster had changed from his eye-catching circus outfit into a sober suit of brown tweed, and he wore a dark brown bowler on his head. He went on, "You know why I'm here."

"I was expecting you," Travis replied. "I've sent Cody to fetch Thurman Simpson. We'll get to the bottom of this business about the horse being shot." The marshal went behind his desk again and sat down, gesturing for Jeffries to take a seat opposite him. "I don't suppose Cahoon showed up out at your camp after Cody and I left, did he?"

Jeffries shook his head. "That obnoxious young man did not put in another appearance, for which we may all be thankful. Are there many such troublemakers here in Kansas, Marshal?"

"We've got more than our share." Travis sighed. "There are plenty of cowhands who decided driving cattle was too much work, like Cahoon. Plus we've got all kinds of drifters and criminals from back East. A lot of them are just passing through on their way to California."

Jeffries sniffed. "I suppose there are men everywhere who have to muddy the waters, so to speak."

"Everywhere I've been," Travis agreed. He spotted two figures passing the window on the boardwalk outside. "Speaking of whom . . ."

Cody opened the door and stepped back to let Thurman Simpson precede him. "Go right on in, Mr. Simpson," the deputy said. "Marshal Travis is waiting to talk to you."

Simpson stalked into the office, glanced at Jeffries, then confronted Travis with an angry look on his face. "See here, Marshal," he snapped, "I demand to know what this is all about! Your deputy comes dragging me out of my house in the middle of the night—"

"Take it easy, Mr. Simpson," Travis cut in. "Have a seat. There's just a little matter that needs clearing up."

Simpson glanced at Jeffries again as if wondering who he was, and then he reluctantly sat down in the chair Cody shoved up behind him.

Travis clasped his hands together on top of the desk and asked, "Where were you late this afternoon, Mr. Simpson?"

Simpson frowned. "Why, I was at the school all afternoon. Where else would I be?"

"The children are finished for the day at three o'clock, isn't that right?"

"Yes, it is."

"Was anybody else there besides you after that?"

"No, I was working alone—" Simpson broke off and stared suspiciously at Travis. "Why are you questioning me? Who is this man?"

"You do not recognize me, sir?" Jeffries asked.

Simpson shook his head. "You look familiar, but no, I don't place you."

Travis performed the introductions. "Mr. Simpson, this is Professor Jericho Jeffries."

"The man from the circus!" Simpson exclaimed.

"And I know all too well who you are," Jeffries said coldly. "You, sir, are the man who shot a defenseless horse."

Simpson's eyes widened in a stunned stare. "What?" he gasped.

Travis leaned forward, wishing that Jeffries had let him handle this in his own way. But it was too late for that now. He glanced at Cody and saw the smile on the young man's face. Cody was enjoying this.

"The horse that you had that run-in with this morning during the parade has been shot and killed," Travis said. "It happened out at the circus camp sometime this afternoon."

"Well, I certainly had nothing to do with it!" Simpson declared. He glowered at Jeffries. "And I resent being accused of such a thing!"

Travis opened the drawer of his desk and took out the small pistol that had been found at the scene. He pushed it across the desk toward the schoolteacher. "Take a look at this, Mr. Simpson," he said. "Is that your gun?"

Simpson picked up the Allen and Thurber .34, which Travis had unloaded earlier. "It's not mine," he said flatly. "I've never even seen a gun like this, to tell you the truth."

"It's a pepperbox," Cody put in, leaning a hip on the corner of the desk. "The kind of a gun that a city feller would carry."

Simpson frowned up at him. "I tell you, it's not mine."

"Look at the grip," Travis suggested quietly.

Simpson's normally pale skin blanched as he saw the name carved in the wooden grip. "I . . . I don't understand," he began.

Jeffries slapped the desk with an open palm. "Well, I understand perfectly!" he roared. "You came out to the circus and shot that horse, you . . . you sour-faced pedagogue, and I intend to see you in jail for it!"

"Hold on!" Travis said, coming to his feet.

Simpson quivered with anger as he scraped his chair back and stood up. "I won't tolerate this!" he said. "It's perfectly clear, Marshal. Someone out at that circus killed the horse and is trying to cast the blame on me. They put my name on this gun!"

"You blithering idiot!" Jeffries shot back. "Why the devil would any of my people do that?"

Simpson shrugged his narrow shoulders. "How should I know? Who knows why you degenerates do the things you do?"

"Degenerates?" Jeffries howled. He took a step toward Simpson.

Travis came out from behind the desk and moved smoothly between the two furious men. "Both of you shut up!" he snapped. Glancing at the grinning Cody, he went on, "And if you're not too busy enjoying yourself, Deputy, you might give me a hand here."

"Sure thing, Marshal." Cody put a hand on Simpson's shoulder and drew him back. "Just sit back down like a good boy," Cody told him, giving him a slight shove into the chair.

"You, too, Professor," Travis said to Jeffries. "Sit down and keep that temper of yours under control."

"Very well," Jeffries sniffed. He sat stiffly in the ladder-backed chair.

Travis turned back to Simpson. "Professor Jeffries does have a point," he said. "Nobody with the circus would have a motive for killing the horse, at least not as far as I can see. And you did threaten the animal, Mr. Simpson."

Simpson shook his head. "I was just angry at the time. I had nothing to do with this." As nervousness replaced the anger in his eyes, it was plain that the schoolteacher was beginning to realize he might be in serious trouble.

Coldly, Jeffries said, "If you didn't do it, and none of my people did, then who do you suggest is the culprit?"

Simpson looked from Travis to the ringmaster, then back to the marshal. "I . . . I don't know. Perhaps, uh, perhaps one of my students . . . Yes, that could be it!" He shook a finger in the air. "You know how some of those children like to cause trouble, Marshal Travis. Why, only yesterday two of them tried to burn down the entire town!"

Cody grunted. "Hector and Johnny wouldn't kill a horse. They're good kids."

"They're hooligans!" Simpson insisted.

Travis shook his head dubiously. "That doesn't sound very likely to me, Mr. Simpson, but I suppose I can look into that angle. For the moment, though, I don't have any choice but to regard you as the main suspect in this business."

"What . . . what are you going to do?"

"Professor Jeffries here wants me to arrest you," Travis said blandly.

Simpson turned toward Jeffries. "You have to be reasonable, man. I'm innocent, but even so, if I'm thrown into jail I'll be ruined. I'm a schoolteacher. I can't allow even a hint of wrongdoing!"

Jeffries grimaced as he pondered the situation. Finally, he said, "I don't want a scandal. Even though I consider you one of the most reprehensible individuals I have ever met, sir, I am willing to forgo any legal action if you'll make appropriate restitution."

"What'd he say?" Cody asked.

"He wants Mr. Simpson here to pay for the horse," Travis told him.

"That's right," Jeffries confirmed. "Since I suppose you were provoked, Simpson, if you'll simply pay for the horse, I'll drop any formal complaint. I believe one hundred dollars should cover it."

"But . . . but . . ." Simpson's face was darkening with anger again. "But I'm innocent! I refuse to pay this . . . this extortion!"

"Then I shall file a complaint, and you, sir, will be jailed. Isn't that correct, Marshal?"

Travis sighed. "I would have to take some sort of action if the professor files an official complaint, Mr. Simpson."

Simpson's face grew bleak as the seriousness of his problem finally sunk in. "I don't have any choice, do I?" he grated.

"We've all got choices," Travis said. "It's just that sometimes we don't like any of them."

"All right," Simpson said savagely. "I'll pay. But I still say I had nothing to do with any of this. And I insist that you continue your investigation, Marshal," he told Travis, who nodded in reply.

Jeffries stood up. "I'm glad you came to your senses, sir. I don't imagine you have that much cash with you, eh?"

Simpson shook his head and said, "I'll have to go to the bank in the morning. Is that all right?"

"That will do nicely. You can give the money to the marshal here, and he can deliver it to me later. Is that satisfactory, Marshal?"

Travis nodded. "Fine by me."

Simpson pushed his chair back and stood up. "This is not right," he declared. "I've done nothing wrong. But you'll have your blood money tomorrow, Jeffries."

With that, he turned on his heel and stalked out of the office.

"Quite an unpleasant chap, isn't he?" Jeffries asked.

Travis was not very happy to have been placed in this position by the ringmaster. He ignored Jeffries's comment and said, "I'll bring the money with me when I ride out for tomorrow night's performance."

"Excellent. I'll see you then, Marshal. Good night."

When Jeffries was gone, Cody looked at Travis and said, "I thought the fur was really going to fly for a while there. Maybe we should've let them fight it out, Marshal. Might've been interesting."

Travis sat down behind his desk and grunted. "It's been a long day. Why don't you go get some sleep?"

"I'll just do that." Cody grinned. "Reckon I'll dream about that sharpshootin' gal?"

"I wouldn't be surprised," Travis told him.

IX

A three-quarter moon floated in the dark Kansas sky, casting its cold light over the quiet circus camp. The hour was late, and although some of the animals were still awake, the human occupants were sleeping. Several of the big cats paced back and forth in their wagons, their instincts telling them that they should be out on the hunt.

A figure slipped from shadow to shadow, moving soundlessly. In the brief moments when the figure was illuminated by the moonlight, it resolved itself into a human shape. The figure glided past the darkened wagons where the members of the troupe slept. He was heading for the animal cages.

As the figure flitted past a wagon where a tiger prowled restlessly, the big cat growled. The intruder ignored the sound, not stopping at these wagons. Instead, he went to the area where the cages containing the smaller animals were kept. There were monkeys and bear cubs and several kinds of exotic birds. The man went from cage to cage, unlatching the doors and swinging them wide open. The dozing animals watched him sleepily but did not try to escape from the now-open cages. They were accustomed to the enclosures and regarded them as home.

When he finished this part of his mission, the intruder moved stealthily toward the compound where the largest animals were penned. He paused at the makeshift fence, regarding the shadowy bulks of the elephants, camels, and zebras. The animals were all tied to stakes driven in the ground. The ropes were what actually held them; the flimsy fence would not stop a charge.

The man opened the gate into the compound, and its hinges gave a slight squeak as it swung back. Stepping inside, the intruder went first to one of the zebras. He slipped a knife from inside his coat and bent to slash the rope.

"Hey! What the hell are you doing?"

The intruder spun around and straightened, bringing the knife up. He spotted one of the roustabouts hurrying toward him. A low-pitched curse ripped from him. This was damned bad luck. The roustabout must have been sleeping somewhere on the ground nearby and had been awakened by the noise of the gate opening.

"Get away from those animals!" the roustabout called. He stopped short as he saw the intruder's face in the moonlight. "You!" he said in surprise.

The shadowed figure waved the knife in his hand menacingly. "Get out of here, Burt!" he warned. "This is none of your business!"

The roustabout looked over the intruder's shoulder and saw that the zebra's tether had been cut. "You're turnin' the animals loose!" he exclaimed. "You gone crazy."

"I'm warning you, Burt—"

"Damn you!" the roustabout grated, leaping at the man with the knife.

The man tried to get out of the way, but Burt grabbed his arm, driving the knife aside, and barreled into him. Both men fell, rolling toward the animals and making the zebras and camels shy away.

The intruder tore away from the roustabout's grasp and sprang to his feet, realizing suddenly that the knife was no longer in his hand. Looking down, he saw moonlight reflecting on the handle; he realized with a start that the blade was buried hilt-deep just under Burt's rib cage. The roustabout was motionless, his eyes staring blankly at the sky as a large dark stain spread across his chest.

Kneeling beside Burt's body, the man pulled his lips back from his teeth in a grimace and muttered, "I-I'm sorry . . . I didn't mean . . . "

He stopped. Burt could not hear him. And it did not matter now. The damage was done. All he could do was continue with his original plan.

Grasping the knife, the man pulled it free,

wincing at the sucking sound of the blade leaving the wound. He stood up and moved quickly, going from one stake to another and cutting the ropes with the bloodstained knife. When he had freed all of the large beasts, he lifted the body of the roustabout under the arms, hauled him out of the compound, and concealed the corpse in the shadows of an empty wagon.

The man replaced the knife inside his coat and took out a small pistol. Aiming over the heads of the animals, he fired the pistol three times. The sharp cracks sent the animals surging toward the other side of the compound. The fence sagged, then collapsed, as their weight pressed against it, and suddenly the elephants, camels, and zebras were free. The man lifted his voice in a shout and emptied the other three shots in his gun. Behind him, the smaller animals, driven into a frenzy by the noise, bolted from the cages he had opened earlier. In front of him, the massive elephants started running away from the destroyed compound, followed closely by the camels and zebras. They were running east in a mad rush—toward Abilene.

With a faint smile on his face, the intruder faded into the shadows as shouts of alarm began to rise from the camp.

It had been a long day, Luke Travis thought as he stepped up onto the boardwalk in front of his office. A damn long day, what with the circus parade, the trouble with Ned Cahoon, the situation with Thurman Simpson and the clown's horse, and everything else that had happened.

He had just completed his final rounds for the night. For the most part Abilene was quiet, although some of the saloons on Texas Street and Railroad Street were still going strong. Travis was ready for some sleep, and he was going to turn in as soon as possible.

Something made him pause, some flicker of motion barely glimpsed in the dim light cast by the streetlamps and the moon. Turning, he leaned one hand on a post supporting the awning over the boardwalk, and his eyes narrowed as he studied the street. A large hump-backed animal ran past him, its hooves thundering like a horse's.

Travis stared, then shook his head. Was he so tired he was seeing things? If that was the case, then he supposed he was imagining the monkey that suddenly scurried past his feet.

Travis reacted instinctively, drawing his gun and lining its sights before he realized he was about to blast a chimpanzee. He held his finger off the trigger and glanced at the street as more hoofbeats drew his attention. A zebra galloped by, its stripes flickering in the moonlight.

Then came the most awesome sight of all. Ears flapping, their trunks lifted as they trumpeted their alarm, four elephants rumbled down Texas Street in full stampede.

"Cody!" Travis yelled at the top of his lungs. He spun to the door of the office and flung it open.

The shout made Cody Fisher rise straight up off the cot where he slept in the back room of the office. His holster and shell belt were hung from a peg beside the cot, and he snagged the Colt on his way up. Landing on his feet, he lunged through the door into the office and saw Travis framed in the entrance.

"Get out here!" Travis barked. The elephants trumpeted again, and Cody's eyes widened in shock at the unfamiliar noise.

When the deputy had joined him on the boardwalk, Travis pointed at the elephants as they charged by. "You see that?" Travis demanded.

"What the hell!" Cody shouted. "It's the damn elephants!"

Travis nodded. Another camel trotted by, following the elephants, and it glanced in their direction, its gaze baleful. "That whole damned circus menagerie must've gotten loose," Travis said. "Get your pants on. We'd best start rounding them up."

Cody looked down, realizing he was clad only in his long johns. He shook his head and said, "Marshal, just how do you round up an elephant, anyway?"

"Same way as you do a cow—I hope." Travis holstered his gun. "I'll get some help."

While Cody ducked into the office, Travis ran down the boardwalk past Aileen Bloom's office to Orion's Tavern. Several men were standing in front of the Scotsman's saloon, looking up the street with stunned expressions on their faces.

"Wha' the bloody hell was tha', Lucas?" Orion demanded as Travis pounded up to them. "Sounded like the skirling o' the bagpipes o' hell, it did!"

"Elephants," Travis said simply. "They've escaped from the circus, along with

Lord knows what else. You men come with me, and we'll start rounding them up."

One of the men held up his hands and started backing away. "I ain't no elephant-puncher, Marshal," he protested. None of his companions looked very enthusiastic about the idea, either.

"I'll help ye, Lucas," Orion declared. "The beast ain't been born tha' Orion McCarthy kinna handle."

"Come on then." With Orion at his side, Travis started back up the street, following in the wake of the runaway animals. Other men were pouring out of the open saloons.

Cody hurried from the office in time to nearly trip over a small, furry form. He caught himself, reached down, and picked up a bear cub. Holding the cub up so that Travis could see it, Cody called, "What'll I do with this one, Marshal?"

"Put it in a cell," Travis told him. "That's about all we can do with the smaller animals."

Cody grinned and turned back into the office. "Come on, you hairy little desperado."

Within minutes, the onslaught of the circus animals had thrown the town into chaos. Travis ran from place to place, accompanied by Orion, as shouts of surprise and fear told them where the beasts were. Lights began being lit all over Abilene as the commotion spread.

On the outskirts of town, in the parsonage of the Calvary Methodist Church, the Reverend Judah Fisher heard the uproar as he worked in his study on his next sermon. He was in shirt-sleeves, his tie loose around his neck. Frowning, he stood up and went to the open window, peering through it toward downtown.

There was a soft knock on the study door. Judah called, "Come in," and Sister Laurel opened the door.

"Several of the children were awakened by that commotion in town, Reverend," the nun said. "Can you tell what it is?"

Gunshots rang out, followed by whoops and shouts. Judah shook his head. "I'm not sure," he said, "but whatever it is, it certainly has the town aroused."

"I'm afraid that now most of the children are awake and curious. I left Agnes to watch them, but I'm sure they won't settle down until we know what is going on."

Judah nodded. "I'll go check. It sounds as if my help might be needed, anyway."

As he shrugged into his coat and left the parsonage to get his horse from the stable, a smaller figure darted after him. "Wait up, Pastor!" Michael Hirsch called. "Take me with you."

Judah turned to face the boy. "I most certainly will not. I'm not going to take a young boy into what might be bad trouble." The minister frowned. "I thought you were supposed to be with your sister and the others."

"Aw, Agnes thinks a person should run and hide whenever anything good happens. Sister Laurel, too. They already chewed my—yelled at me for getting back late from the circus."

Judah tried not to grin. "Go on inside, Michael," he said firmly. "I'll tell you all about it when I get back."

Grumbling, Michael turned toward the parsonage, and Judah went into the stable to get his horse. A few moments later he rode quickly down Elm Street toward the main section of Abilene.

He did not notice the boyish figure hurrying on foot after him, staying in the shadows.

Travis had gathered quite a force of would-be animal handlers, but so far they had not been very successful at recapturing the escaped beasts. All of the zebras had been hazed toward the livery stable, where they were now corraled, but the other animals were still running loose. Cody's bear cub was the only other captive.

It was all so damned ludicrous, Travis thought as he watched Orion chasing a monkey past the Bull's Head Saloon. Where were the people from the circus? They ought to be here helping to clean up this mess. So far, Judah Fisher was the only one helping who had not been in the saloons when the stampede started.

Orion came down the boardwalk toward him carrying the monkey. It was screeching and trying to twist around in his grip so that it could bite him. Gritting his teeth, the tavern keeper said, "I'd be obliged if ye'd take this creature off me hands, Lucas."

"Bring him into the jail," Travis said.

They locked the monkey in the cell next to the one occupied by the bear cub. Maybe they would not fight through the bars, Travis thought. At any rate, this was the best he could do. Travis pushed his hat back and wiped sweat from his forehead with his sleeve.

Whoever was responsible for this little escapade was going to have a lot of explaining to do. Somebody was going to *pay*.

Crouching in the shadows of a storefront on Texas Street, Michael Hirsch thought that he had never had such an exciting night in his life. First the actual performance of the circus, next his meeting the clown Andy, then the job hauling water for the animals, and now this—elephants on the loose in Abilene! He could barely believe his eyes.

Getting into trouble with Agnes and Sister Laurel had been worth it, since he had gotten to stay at the circus camp after the performance and work with the animals. He knew they would be angry with him again for slipping away from the orphanage, but this was going to be worth it, too!

Now he watched as riders tried to turn a camel toward the livery stable. The funny-looking animal did not want to go, and so far it had eluded its pursuers. Michael laughed as he watched the antics, until the sound of frenzied barking drew his attention.

He looked down the street and saw one of the mongrel dogs that frequented the alleys behind the saloons. The dog was in the middle of the street now, and lumbering toward it was one of the elephants. The dog was either too scared or too stubborn to move, because it was standing its ground and yapping at the approaching behemoth.

Acting without thinking, Michael came to his feet. He ran down the boardwalk, then leaped into the street and dashed toward the dog. The elephant was only a few feet away when Michael reached the small animal. He scooped up the barking dog and threw himself to the side. Michael felt the earth shake beneath him as the elephant thundered by in the dusty street. Releasing the squirming dog, he rolled over on his hands and knees to watch as it tore away, its tail between its legs.

Stupid dog! It had almost gotten him killed—

"Look out, kid!"

The frightened cry made Michael's head jerk up. A camel had broken away from the men trying to capture it, and it was galloping down Texas Street straight at him. The ugly, awkward-looking beast was anything but slow and clumsy now as it raced toward him.

Michael's eyes widened in horror. He

knew he would never be able to get out of the way in time.

A man on horseback came out of an alley a few feet away. Digging his heels into the flanks of his mount, the man held on as the horse lunged forward. Deputy Cody Fisher leaned far over in his saddle to grab Michael's belt and lift him into the air. Cody's horse leaped out of the way as the camel went crashing by.

Cody lifted Michael and dropped him into the saddle in front of him. "Don't know what the hell you're doing here, Michael," the deputy said, "but you'd better stay up here with me, out of the way, until we get these animals penned up."

"Sure, Cody," Michael said breathlessly, his heart still pounding from his close brush with catastrophe. The only thing that could have improved this night was to ride with his hero, Cody Fisher. "Thanks for saving my life," he went on.

Cody grinned. "I was just postponing things. I knew Agnes and Sister Laurel would be madder'n hell if I let that camel stomp you before they could get hold of you."

Michael gulped. Cody was right about that.

It was long past midnight, and Travis still had quite a mess to clean up. Jeffries, the roustabouts, and the animal handlers had finally arrived from the circus, and with the help of the townspeople, all of the beasts had been recaptured. They were being taken back to the circus encampment now, and Abilene was settling down in an effort to salvage what was left of the night.

Travis followed the men and animals across the prairie to the camp. He wanted to be certain there were no more mishaps on the way. He also had a few things to say to Professor Jericho Jeffries.

The camp was ablaze with light as Travis approached. Several roustabouts held torches while others worked with the animals. The smaller animals were being put back in their cages, and the elephants, camels, and zebras were tied once more to their stakes. Travis spotted Jeffries near the corral, supervising as some of the roustabouts tried to repair the trampled fence.

"Ah, there you are, Marshal," Jeffries hailed him. "I was hoping you'd come out here. I want to talk to you."

"Not as much as I want to talk to you," Travis said as he swung down from his saddle. Angrily, he continued. "This is just the kind of thing I was afraid would happen when I heard your circus was coming."

Jeffries frowned. "Really, Marshal, you can't blame this on us."

"No? Then whose fault is it those animals terrorized my town and nearly trampled some folks?"

Jeffries held up a piece of rope, one end of it cut cleanly. "It's the fault of whatever villain released them, Marshal. All of the ropes holding the larger animals were cut, and the cages containing the smaller ones were opened."

Travis reached out and took the rope from Jeffries. Studying the end in the light from a nearby torch, he saw it had indeed been cut. He glanced up at the ringmaster. "There's no way those monkeys are agile enough to let themselves out?"

Jeffries shook his head. "The cages are designed to prevent just such an occurrence. No, Marshal, this was sabotage."

Travis started to ask who would do such a thing, but before he could say a word, a scream ripped through the torchlit night. Both lawman and ringmaster whirled around as a woman came stumbling out from behind a nearby wagon. Travis recognized her as the female member of the trick-riding team. She had her hands pressed to her mouth, and now she took them away to cry, "It's Burt! Somebody's killed Burt!"

Jeffries caught her arm. "What? Where is he?"

The woman pointed shakily toward the shadows beside the wagon. "O-over there," she quavered.

Travis and Jeffries exchanged a look, then Travis started toward the wagon. Jeffries handed the shaken woman over to one of the other performers and followed the marshal.

Passing one of the roustabouts carrying a torch, Travis reached out and took the blazing brand from him. He turned toward the wagon and lifted the torch so that the shadows fell away.

An unmistakable air of death hung about the sprawled body on the ground next to the wagon. "It's Burt, all right," Jeffries said from behind him as they knelt beside the body. "He's one of the roustabouts. My God, what happened?"

Travis studied the bloody shirt for a moment, then pulled it back to reveal the thin wound. "Looks like somebody stuck a knife in him," Travis grunted.

Jeffries shuddered and ran a hand over his beard. "Who would do such a monstrous thing?"

"Did this fellow usually stay out here close to the animals at night?"

Jeffries nodded. "He was fond of the camels, of all things. Filthy beasts, they are."

"He probably saw whoever was turning them loose," Travis mused. "He tried to stop it and got a knife for his trouble." The marshal glanced up at Jeffries, and his eyes were bleak. "You and I have got to have a long talk, mister."

"Yes," Jeffries said absently. He was obviously shaken by the violence. "Yes, I believe we should."

One of the roustabouts was sent into Abilene on horseback to fetch the undertaker. Jeffries called a tall, burly bald man over to the wagon and said, "Bruno, will you keep an eye on poor Burt's body until someone from town comes for it?"

Travis recognized Bruno as the circus strong man. Bruno nodded, a solemn expression on his face. "Sure, Professor," he said. "What happened, anyway?"

"I hope we can figure that out, Bruno," Jeffries said wearily. Turning to Travis, he went on. "Why don't we go back to my wagon for our discussion, Marshal?"

"All right with me," Travis said. "Lead the way."

The two men made their way through the confusion of the camp to Jeffries's wagon. Once inside, Jeffries lit an oil lantern. His face was a haggard mask as he sank down wearily in a chair and rubbed his eyes. After a moment, he looked up and said, "I'm being a poor host. Would you like a drink, Marshal?"

Travis shook his head. "No, thanks," he said curtly. He was looking around the inside of the wagon, surprised that it offered as much comfort as it did. There were several chairs, a table, a good-sized bunk, and a thick rug on the floor. The walls were decorated with circus posters, handbills much like the ones that Gil Palmer had tacked up all over Abilene. The colorful sheets advertised not only Jeffries's own show but other traveling circuses as well. It was a very masculine place, and Travis supposed that Jeffries had changed it after the death of his wife. The man probably did not want to be surrounded by reminders of her.

"Quite an evening, eh?" Jeffries asked,

chuckling humorlessly. "I daresay you'll be glad to see us go, Marshal."

"Not until we've got this murder cleared up, not to mention all the other trouble you've had."

"Ah, yes, trouble. We've had more than our share, I have to admit that." Jeffries's self-assurance seemed to have deserted him. "I don't mind telling you, sir, that we have been plagued by problems for months now."

Travis turned a chair around and straddled it, his interest quickening. "What kind of problems?"

"Well, we've had quite a few vehicles break down, as I believe I mentioned to you. There have also been instances where funds have turned up missing."

"Somebody's been stealing from you?"

Jeffries nodded. "Indeed. And there was a small fire that destroyed some of our equipment a few weeks ago. Never anything too serious, mind you. Certainly no one's life has ever been in danger, like poor Burt's was tonight."

"That was bad luck," Travis said, pushing his hat to the back of his head as he thought about what Jeffries was telling him. "If he hadn't come along when he did, nothing would have happened except that the animals would have gotten loose. That posed a problem in town, but I'm starting to think that whoever's behind your problems didn't intend to kill anybody. After all, none of the really dangerous animals were let loose."

"I can't understand why anyone would want to cause trouble for the circus—unless, of course, it's that fellow who interrupted Dorinda's act tonight."

Travis rubbed his jaw and hesitated for a moment before voicing the thought that was on his mind. Then he said, "Ned Cahoon could be involved, but that wouldn't explain your other troubles. Let me ask you—could your wife's accident have been part of all this, Professor?"

Jeffries blinked, old pain flaring in his eyes. "How . . . How do you know about my wife, Marshal?"

"Gil Palmer told me. He had an accident, too. Could he and your wife have both been victims of this mysterious troublemaker?"

Jeffries shook his head emphatically. "I assure you, Marshal, both of those horrible incidents were completely accidental. They were similar in nature, in fact. In both cases, a somersault was mistimed. The catcher was in position, but Gil and Mary both failed to reach him. If there is any blame to be attached to their tragedies, it must go to me for not insisting that they use nets."

"Palmer said the acrobats didn't want the nets, even after he was hurt."

Jeffries shrugged his shoulders. His eyes were damp now. "I should have insisted."

Travis sat there watching the ringmaster for a moment. Jeffries's face was downcast, and his sorrow and regret certainly seemed genuine.

Before Travis could say anything else, someone banged on the door of the wagon. Cody Fisher called, "Marshal? You in there?"

Travis stood up and opened the door. Cody stood there, the splash of lanternlight from inside the wagon revealing his tense face.

"You all right, Marshal?" Cody asked.

"Sure. What are you doing out here, Cody?"

"I rode out with Worden, the undertaker. One of the roustabouts came into town and said somebody'd been killed out here. I thought I'd better see what it was about." Cody looked past Travis and saw Jeffries sitting with his hands over his eyes. "Is he all right?"

His voice low, Travis quickly explained

what had happened. Cody nodded in under-standing. Travis finished by saying, "It looks to me like someone who is traveling with the circus is out to destroy it."

"That seems more and more likely." A worried expression crept over Cody's lean face. "Have you seen Miss Russell since you came back out here, Marshal?"

Travis thought for a moment, then shook his head. "No, I don't believe I have."

"If it's all right with you, I think I'll go check on her—just in case Ned Cahoon *was* involved."

The marshal nodded. "Probably a good idea. I want to talk to Jeffries some more, see what he thinks about the idea that he's got a traitor in his troupe. I'll be here for a while."

Cody moved off into the darkness, search-ing for Dorinda Russell's wagon. He asked a passing roustabout for directions, and a few minutes later he was knocking on the door of a small, nondescript wagon. Evi-dently Dorinda saved all the fancy frills for her act.

"Who is it?" a female voice called from inside.

"Deputy Cody Fisher, Miss Dorinda."

The door swung open. Dorinda brushed

a strand of chestnut hair from her face and smiled sleepily at him. "Hello, Deputy. What brings you out here in the middle of the night?"

"You mean you didn't hear all the ruckus when the animals escaped?"

Dorinda nodded. "Of course I did. I started to go into town with the others to help round them up, but Professor Jeffries told me to stay here, that I wouldn't be needed. I'm afraid I went back to sleep." She was wearing a robe belted tightly around her trim waist.

"Then you don't know about the killing."

Dorinda's eyes widened. "Someone was killed by the animals?" she asked incredulously.

Cody shook his head. "Not unless one of the monkeys can handle a knife. One of the roustabouts, a fellow named Burt, was stabbed by whoever turned the animals loose. At least that's the way Marshal Travis has it figured."

"My God," Dorinda breathed. "Poor Burt. Does the marshal have any idea who's responsible?"

Cody shrugged. He was not sure whether Travis would want him going into the theory that one of the members of the troupe was guilty. "He'll get it sorted out sooner or later," Cody said instead. "But I just wanted to make sure you were all right, Miss Russell."

She came down a step and smiled at him. "I thought you were going to call me Dorinda. And I'm fine, Cody. I appreciate you worrying about me."

As Cody looked up at her in the light from a nearby torch, he thought she was still the most beautiful woman he had ever seen. Even wearing a robe, with her hair tousled from sleep, she was lovely. Peering into her brown eyes, he felt a tingle run up his spine. He wondered if she was feeling the same thing.

Suddenly at a loss for words, he touched the brim of his hat and said, "I—I'd better get back to the marshal. There might be something he wants me to do."

Dorinda reached out and lightly touched his arm. "Thank you for coming by to see about me."

Cody swallowed. He was going to pull this woman into his arms and kiss her in about ten seconds—if he did not get out of here first. "Be seein' you," he muttered as he turned away quickly.

212

Heading across the camp toward Jeffries's wagon, he pushed Dorinda from his mind by mulling over Travis's theory. By the time Cody reached the ringmaster's wagon, Travis had explained his speculation to Jeffries, and the idea had met with resistance.

"Absolutely not!" Jeffries insisted. "These people are my family. None of them would try to hurt me or the circus!"

"Somebody's got it in for you," Travis said grimly.

Jeffries shook his head. "Impossible! At least none of my people. It must be that Ned Cahoon fellow. Or that schoolteacher of yours."

The door of the wagon was open, and the deputy arrived in time to hear the last of the conversation. Pausing in the doorway, Cody said, "The professor may be right, Marshal, at least about tonight's incident. Ned Cahoon's sure as hell got a grudge against the circus after Dorinda put him in his place. He would turn those animals loose and kill that roustabout."

Travis frowned. It was true that Ned Cahoon was a likely suspect in this trouble, but it still seemed to him that one of the circus people was behind it. They could not afford to overlook any possibilities, however.

"Find out where Cahoon went tonight after the show," he told Cody. "I want to know if he has an alibi for the time of the killing."

Cody grinned. "You bet."

Travis turned back to Jeffries. "I'll be keeping an eye on this place, Jeffries. Maybe we can head off any more trouble before it happens. But my main responsibility is keeping the peace in Abilene."

"I understand, Marshal," Jeffries said. His voice became grim as he went on. "Whoever our culprit is, we shall find him. Find him . . . and deal with him."

X

Walking wearily across Texas street, Travis squinted in the bright morning sunlight. After only two hours' sleep, his eyes were gritty, his shoulders ached. He hoped that a cup of strong black coffee would help to clear the fog of fatigue that had wrapped itself around him. As he opened the door into the Sunrise Café, he dropped his head to loosen the tight muscles in his neck and walked directly into a surprised patron who was leaving just as Travis was entering.

"Palmer," Travis said with a start.

Gil Palmer, who had recovered from the collision by grasping at a chair directly behind him, turned to smile at Travis. "Good morning, Marshal. You look a bit out of sorts this morning."

Travis grimaced. "It was a long night."

"I heard about the animals escaping. Sounds like quite an adventure."

"Quite a mess, you mean," Travis said. He frowned. "What are you still doing in Abilene? I thought you had moved on to Dodge or Hays or Wichita with those handbills of yours."

Palmer leaned against the chair. "I would have if the circus had kept to its original schedule," he explained. "But since Professor Jeffries decided to stay here for a few days, I decided it was a good opportunity to have my team of horses reshod. The circus is nearly always on the go, and I like to rest my animals and take care of them whenever I can."

Travis nodded in understanding. "Sounds like a good idea." He waved a hand toward a vacant table. "Had breakfast already?"

"Just finished."

"Could I talk you into another cup of coffee?"

Palmer grinned. "I think you could do that, Marshal."

While they spoke, Travis had decided to question Palmer about the problems that had been plaguing the circus. Strictly speaking, he was still a member of the troupe, but he was on the outside to a certain extent and might have a different perspective on events.

"Good morning, Marshal," Agnes Hirsch said as Travis and Palmer sat down at the table. She, too, looked bleary-eyed this morning. "Did Cody tell you about what Michael did last night?"

Travis tried not to grin. "Yes, he mentioned it. Said Michael nearly got trampled by an elephant and a camel. Knowing that brother of yours, it doesn't surprise me." More seriously he added, "I'm glad he wasn't hurt."

"When Sister Laurel and Reverend Fisher finished giving him a talking-to, I think he wished he was back with the wild animals," Agnes replied with a slight grin.

Gil Palmer frowned. "You mean some child was almost killed during all the excitement?"

"That's right." Travis nodded. "That was the closest we came to having any injuries here in town. Agnes, how about a stack of hotcakes and plenty of bacon? And keep the coffee coming. Bring Mr. Palmer a cup, too."

"Sure, Marshal." The pretty young redhead turned toward the kitchen to pass the order on to the cook.

Agnes set cups of coffee down in front of the two men a moment later. Travis sipped the steaming brew and felt some strength flowing back into his veins. "I guess you heard about what happened out at the circus camp."

"You mean about that roustabout getting killed?" Palmer's face was now grim. "Yes, I did. Do you have any idea who did it, Marshal?"

Travis shook his head. "The way I figure it, whoever turned the animals loose did the killing, too. The roustabout must have spotted him in the act."

"I certainly hope you find whoever is responsible."

"The fellow who was killed was a friend of yours, eh?"

Palmer shrugged. "Not particularly. But the circus is more than a job; it's a family.

217

us."

"Seems like a lot of bad things have been happening to Jeffries's circus lately," Travis mused. "You have any ideas about that?"

Palmer looked shrewdly at the marshal. "Are you talking about the professor's financial troubles?"

"Didn't know he was having any," Travis replied honestly. "According to Jeffries, somebody's been sabotaging the show for the last several months."

"I wouldn't know anything about that. Oh, I had heard that they were having some trouble with wagons breaking down. And then there was that fire a few weeks back. . . ." Palmer's voice trailed off as a thoughtful expression came over his face. "You know, I had never really thought about it, but I believe you're right, Marshal. Too many things have been happening for all of them to be coincidence."

"That's what I think," Travis agreed. "Now, what were you saying about money troubles?"

Palmer leaned forward. "Now that I think about it, the whole thing could be connected. The circus's profits have been way down so far this year. The problem could stem from this sabotage you've been talking about."

"Do you have any idea who could be behind it?"

Palmer thought for a moment, then shook his head. "I'm really not around the circus itself much. I might stay with them a couple of nights a week, but the rest of the time I'm out on the road, traveling ahead of them to drum up interest. The only thing I can think of—" He broke off abruptly and shook his head.

"What?" Travis prodded.

Palmer hesitated. Before he could speak, Agnes appeared with the platter of food for Travis. Palmer sipped from his mug and then shook his head again.

Not touching his food, Travis waited until Agnes was beyond earshot before he probed Palmer. "If you've got a notion of who might be behind this, I want to hear it," Travis insisted.

"It's just that the whole idea is so far-fetched. . . . But I guess you're right. You have to consider everything." Palmer took a deep breath, then plunged ahead. "I've known Jericho Jeffries for a long time, Marshal, and I don't believe he has ever recovered from the death of his wife."

Travis frowned. "What are you saying?"

"Who would be in a better position to cause trouble for the show than the professor himself?"

The blunt question made Travis lean back in his chair, his forehead furrowed. "Why the hell would Jeffries want to hurt his own business?"

"Grief does funny things to a man," Palmer pointed out. "Especially when he loses someone as close to him as a wife."

Palmer's words struck a chord within Travis. He knew from painful experience what losing a wife was like. But Travis's face betrayed none of his feelings; he sat quietly waiting for Palmer to continue.

"Maybe Jericho blames himself for Mary's death," Palmer went on. "Maybe he's trying to punish himself. Could be he's not even fully aware of what he's doing." Palmer spread his hands. "But this is just pointless speculation. Neither one of us really thinks that the professor could be behind the troubles."

"It's not likely," Travis mused. "But it is something to think about. I can't and won't overlook any suspects."

"What about that cowboy who disrupted Dorinda's act? I was at the performance,

220

and I imagine he's holding quite a grudge. I recognized him as the one who picked that fight with me a couple of mornings ago."

Travis nodded. "Ned Cahoon. Yes, we've considered him, all right. Cahoon's the type who wouldn't stop at anything to settle a score. I've got my deputy checking on him."

"There's your villain," Palmer said fervently. "Not Jericho Jeffries."

"You may be right. We'll find out sooner or later. Now, I'm going to eat these hotcakes while they're still hot."

Cody Fisher wearily pushed open the batwing doors of Orion's Tavern and stepped onto the boardwalk. He had spent the morning checking every saloon in Abilene, making his way from large, well-appointed bars like the Bull's Head and the Alamo to hole-in-the-wall dives such as Red Mike's. But they all had one thing in common: Ned Cahoon had not been seen in any of them.

Of course, there was always the chance that he was being lied to, Cody thought as he strolled toward the marshal's office. Most of the bartenders and saloon patrons had little reason to love the law or its representatives. They might play dumb if the notion struck them. Not that long ago, Cody himself had been in a similar situation.

He had been in Dodge City when a gunfight with the notorious Josh Weaver had left Weaver dead and Cody wounded. It had been self-defense—the law was not his pursuer. But Cody was hunted by men wanting to avenge Weaver's death and by young toughs hoping to build a name by outdrawing Weaver's killer.

All that had changed, thanks to Luke Travis and Judah and a few others in Abilene. Cody Fisher had become a guardian of law and order.

There were times when the role chafed him, when he felt an urge to move on to see what was over the next rise. New dangers to be faced, new women to be kissed . . .

Travis looked up from his desk as Cody came into the office. The marshal had his Winchester in his lap and was cleaning the weapon. Only Cody took as good care of his guns.

"You find Cahoon?" Travis asked.

Cody flipped his hat onto the rack just inside the door and shook his head. "Nope. To hear folks around here tell it, Ned Cahoon's dropped off the face of the earth."

Travis grunted. "We couldn't be that lucky."

"I checked all the saloons," Cody said as he sat down in a ladder-backed chair and tilted it against the wall. He balanced himself with one foot against the cold iron stove. "Nobody's seen him, or so they say. I made sure that everyone knew that I wanted to talk to him."

"Do you think it'll do any good?"

Cody shrugged. "I guess that depends on where he shows up next."

Travis nodded. "I saw Gil Palmer this morning," he said, changing the subject.

"That fellow who puts up the posters for the circus? Didn't know he was still around."

"He's getting his team reshod. He's got some interesting ideas about who's trying to wreck Jeffries's show."

"Why, it's Cahoon, of course," Cody said. "Who else could it be?"

"Cahoon didn't cause the wagons to break down hundreds of miles from here," Travis pointed out. "He didn't start a fire over in another state."

Cody frowned and ran a thumb along his jaw. "No, I guess he didn't. But I'd be willing to bet he's the one who killed that jasper and let those creatures loose."

"Could be. But Palmer seems to think Jeffries himself might be causing some of the trouble."

"Jeffries?" Cody exclaimed. "Now that's the dumbest thing I've ever heard. Why the hell would Jeffries want to ruin his own circus?"

"Because he feels guilty over his wife's death. At least that's the theory Palmer gave me. Seems pretty farfetched when you first think about it, but I've seen stranger things happen."

Cody shook his head. "I don't know about all those other things that have happened, but Cahoon's the cause of that ruckus last night, and I'm going to prove it."

The rest of the morning passed quietly. The only official business the two lawmen had to deal with was a merchant's report of a break-in and robbery at his general store. Nothing had been taken except a case of canned peaches. Travis suspected that the stolen goods were already on their way somewhere else in the saddlebags of some cowboys. Few things were more highly prized on the range than canned fruit.

Cody was alone in the office in the early afternoon when hurried footsteps sounded on the boardwalk outside. The door swung open, and a boy about ten years old poked his head in. "You'd best come quick, Deputy!" he said excitedly.

Cody came up out of his chair. "What's the matter?"

The boy shook his head. "Don't know. I was just passin' Orion's place, and he give me a nickel to run down here and fetch you. Said there was somebody there he thought you wanted to see."

Nodding, Cody said, "Thanks." He was already crossing the office and reaching for his hat. The Scotsman had promised to let him know if Ned Cahoon showed up, and Orion kept his word. Cody was sure that that had to be the reason for this summons.

Cody strode quickly down the boardwalk toward Orion's place. He pushed the batwings aside and paused in the entrance of the tavern. Orion was behind the bar, pouring drinks for several cowboys who were leaning on the mahogany. There was a slow-paced poker game going on at one of the tables. At another table in the back of the room a half-dozen men sat nursing drinks. One of them was Ned Cahoon.

Cody studied the situation. Cahoon's two friends were with him, as were three other men of the same stripe. Hardcases, all of them, part of the motley crew that floated through the territory, teaming up from time to time to pull a robbery.

There was a heavy step on the planks behind Cody, and a deep voice said, "Excuse me, mister."

Cody looked around to see the tall, burly form of the circus strong man, Bruno Wagner. "Uh, sure," the deputy said, moving into the saloon.

Bruno went to the bar and nodded to Orion. "Good afternoon, Mr. McCarthy," he said. "I was wondering if you wanted a rematch of that arm wrestling contest."

Old Bailey squawked, "Dinna be daft, man!"

Orion grinned and jerked a thumb at the parrot. "For once in me life, I'm agreeing with tha' bird. I'll be glad t'drink some fine Scotch whisky wi' ye, though."

"Sounds good to me," Bruno declared.

While Orion was pouring the drink, he glanced over Bruno's shoulder and caught Cody's eye, inclining his head toward the table where Cahoon and the others sat. Cody nodded and strolled to the back of the saloon.

Cahoon saw him coming, Cody was sure

of that, but the young man gave no sign of it. He frowned down at his drink until Cody paused by the table and said, "I want to talk to you, Cahoon."

Cahoon raised his eyes and glared at the deputy. "I got nothing to say to you, Fisher."

"I think you do," Cody insisted. Although his attention was centered on Cahoon, he saw that the other men around the table had tensed and were ready for trouble. "I want to ask you some questions."

"Ask all you want, but I'm damned if I'll answer."

"I think you will, unless you want to go down to the jail and talk to the marshal. Where'd you go last night after you left the circus?"

Cahoon's frown deepened. "We went and had some drinks, if it's any of your damned business, which it's not."

"Where?"

"Some saloon." Cahoon shrugged. "I didn't pay much attention. Could've been the Bull's Head or the Silver Dollar or old Tansey's place."

"So you wouldn't be able to produce anybody who could vouch for your whereabouts?"

"We was with him," the one called Dawson spoke up. "We was with him the whole time, wasn't we, Mitch?"

The other one nodded in confirmation.

"You didn't go back to the circus?" Cody prodded.

"Told you I didn't," Cahoon grated. "What is this, Fisher?" A sudden look of realization came over his face. "You think I had something to do with them animals getting loose, don't you?"

"And with a man getting killed," Cody replied. "How about it, Cahoon? Are you sticking with your story?"

"I didn't go near that goddamned circus after I left, and my boys here can back me up. That good enough for you, Deputy?" Cahoon sneered.

Cody laughed shortly. "An alibi like that's not worth a pile of buffalo dung. You'd better not try anything else, Cahoon, because I'm going to keep an eye on you. I haven't forgotten how you tried to ruin Miss Russell's act."

Cahoon tossed off the liquor in his glass and thumped it down on the table. "You warnin' me, Fisher?"

"I sure as hell am."

Cahoon shook his head. "I don't take too

228

kindly to that." Suddenly, he flung the empty glass at Cody's head.

Cody had been expecting it. He dodged aside, the glass missing him by inches. Cahoon exploded out of his chair, overturning the table as he came at Cody with a roar of anger. He threw a roundhouse right with enough steam behind it to take off Cody's head.

The punch never connected. Cody ducked under it, stepped in close, and hooked a right to Cahoon's jaw, knocking him backward. Cahoon stumbled over his chair and fell heavily. As he landed on the floor, he yelled, "Get him!"

Five men surged toward Cody in an angry wave. Undaunted by the odds, Cody lunged toward the man in the center, meeting the charge. As Cody slammed a fist into the man's middle, he heard meaty sounds of knuckles impacting flesh on both sides of him.

"Gang up on the lad, will ye?" Orion McCarthy howled on Cody's right as he rained blows on one of the other hardcases. To the left, Bruno Wagner fought in silence punctuated by a grunt of effort as he picked up two of the men and banged their heads together.

Cahoon was back on his feet, and he threw himself into the fracas. He tackled Cody, driving him backward. Cody's feet went out from under him, and both men fell. They landed on the table where the poker game had been in progress, smashing the table into kindling and scattering money and chips all over the floor. The poker players yelped in protest and scurried out of the way.

Cody slipped out of Cahoon's grasp and clipped him on the jaw with a punch. One of the other men brought a chair crashing down on Orion's head. Orion shook his head, then turned with a shout and laid his hands on the attacker, flinging him over the bar. Bottles shattered as the man smashed into the backbar.

Cody grinned as he saw how Orion had handled the threat, but Cahoon cut short Cody's appreciation by clubbing him from behind with both hands. Cody went down on one knee. Cahoon leaped on his back, looping an arm around the deputy's throat and shutting off his air. Gasping, Cody fell forward, hauling Cahoon over his head. Cahoon slammed to the floor on his back, shaking the planks with the impact of his landing.

Cody rolled over and came to his feet, facing Cahoon as the other man also got up. Cody was aware that Orion and Bruno were at his back, holding off the other members of Cahoon's gang. That left him to deal with Cahoon.

Bigger and heavier than Cody, Cahoon had a longer reach. But Cody was quicker, and the punches that he drove into Cahoon's face stung mercilessly. Cody received several blows to the midsection that threatened to double him over, but he kept to his feet and bored ahead, snapping his fists into Cahoon's solar plexus until Cahoon was set up for the final punch.

Cody put everything he had into the uppercut, timing it perfectly and catching Cahoon on the point of the chin. Cahoon's head jerked up and around, and his eyes rolled up in his head. He swayed for a second, then collapsed bonelessly on the floor.

Breathing heavily and aching all over, Cody turned around to see Orion and Bruno grinning at him. Around them on the floor sprawled the bodies of their opponents. Two of the men were out cold; the other three were moaning and slowly trying to get up.

From the doorway Luke Travis said,

"Well, I see you didn't need my help after all."

"Lucas!" Orion exclaimed. "Ye missed a good fight, man!"

"I can see that," Travis said, nodding. "Looks like quite a bit of damage. Who started it?" He was staring hard at Cody as he asked the question.

"I did, Marshal," Cody said. "I'll pay for the damages." He glanced at Cahoon's still form and went on. "But it was worth it."

"Ye'll do no such," Orion declared. He bent over Cahoon and extracted a couple of bills from inside the man's vest. Looking up at Travis, Orion continued, "Cahoon threw the first punch, Lucas. 'Tis only fair tha' he pay for most o' the damage."

"All right," Travis decided. He turned to Cahoon's friends and told them, "Get him out of here."

"Let me wake him up first," Bruno Wagner said. He got his untouched mug of beer from the bar and dashed the contents in Cahoon's face. Cahoon came up off the floor, blinking and sputtering. Bruno said, "That was probably a waste of good beer."

A couple of Cahoon's companions grabbed his arms and pulled him to his feet. Still sputtering, they led him out of the tavern.

Travis looked at Cody. "Did he have an alibi for last night?"

"Oh, he claimed he was drinking in some saloon. His two sidekicks backed him up. But that doesn't mean anything, Marshal."

"Maybe, maybe not." Travis gestured at Cody's face. "Your mouth's bleeding, you know."

Cody lifted his hand to his mouth and then looked at the crimson on his fingers. He grinned. "Like I said, it was worth it."

XI

Cody held his horse to an easy canter. The spirited pinto preferred a faster pace, but any other gait made Cody wince. Cahoon had lost the fight, but he had been an aggressive opponent, and Cody had taken his share of hard blows. He certainly felt them now. By morning he would be quite stiff, the bruises an angry purple.

As he approached the circus camp, he heard the distinctive pattern of gunfire that told him Dorinda was practicing. As much as he wanted to turn his horse and follow the sound to see her, he knew he had to do his job first. Travis had sent him to the encampment to check that nothing further had gone amiss. Riding away from the gunshots, Cody realized that each day he was taking his work more and more seriously.

Nodding to several performers and roustabouts who greeted him, Cody walked the pinto among the circus wagons until he came to Professor Jericho Jeffries's. He dismounted with a twinge of pain and knocked on the door.

When Jeffries opened it a moment later, he looked haggard, and Cody supposed he had gotten as little sleep as anyone else the night before. "Good afternoon, Deputy," Jeffries said. "What can I do for you?"

"Marshal Travis sent me out to see if there's been any trouble around here today," Cody told him.

"No, thank God. Everything has been quiet." Jeffries gestured at the bruises and scratches on Cody's face. "Bruno Wagner told me about your little set-to with that Cahoon chap. Are you still convinced that he's the one who killed my employee and released the animals?"

"I am," Cody said grimly.

"Then why isn't the man under arrest?"

Cody shook his head. "It's not that easy,

sir. There's a matter of evidence. So far we don't have any against Cahoon."

"Then I suggest you find some before someone else is murdered."

Cody kept his anger in check. Jeffries was tired, and that was probably why he sounded so bitter. "We'll be out here for the performance tonight," the deputy said. "I don't think Cahoon will try anything else for a while."

"I hope not."

Cody said goodbye to the ringmaster and mounted up again, turning his horse toward the clearing where Dorinda practiced at the edge of the camp. As he approached, the guns fell silent, and he spotted the little clown Andy fetching more targets from Dorinda's wagon.

Dorinda was reloading her guns as she stood to one side. Today she wore a butternut shirt and brown whipcord pants. Despite the outfit, there was nothing mannish about her. Her long hair blew gently in the breeze.

"Howdy, ma'am," Cody said, drawing his horse to a halt near her.

"Howdy yourself," Dorinda replied. She glanced up at him, then quickly looked again. "Good Lord," she exclaimed. "What happened to you?"

"Just a difference of opinion." Cody grinned. He found that the bruises did not hurt quite so much, now that Dorinda had noticed them. "I ran into Ned Cahoon this afternoon in town."

"That awful man who tried to ruin my performance?"

"That's the one. I told him to steer clear of the circus, and he took exception to it."

Dorinda slid her right-hand gun into its holster and drew the left-hand Colt. "So the two of you had a fight."

Cody shrugged. "Wasn't much. Just him and a couple dozen of his friends against me. They never stood a chance."

Looking down at the gun she was reloading, Dorinda said, "You must be quite a fighter." There was a slight tone of mockery in her voice.

Cody slid down from the saddle. Yielding to the impulse that had nagged at him since the first time he saw her, he stepped close to her. He quickly slid his arms around her, and as he drew her close to him, her head tilted back. Cody's lips came down on hers in a long, hard kiss. Dorinda's mouth was every bit as warm and sweet as he had expected it to be. She seemed to be enjoying herself as much as he was.

When he finally broke the kiss, Dorinda leaned back in his arms and smiled up at him. "Grabbing a girl with a loaded gun in her hand isn't the smartest thing you could do, Deputy," she said softly.

"I notice you didn't shoot me," Cody pointed out.

"I thought about it. . . ."

Another voice called, "Excuse me, but if you two are through, we've got some work to do, Dorinda."

She smiled as she looked over at Andy. The midget had set up the fresh targets. "You're right, Andy," she told him. To Cody, she said, "You may not have noticed, but your arms are still around me."

"I noticed." He nodded. "You know, I'm surely going to hate it when you leave with the circus."

"Me, too," she replied. "Now that you've been so bold, maybe we'd better take advantage of the time we've got."

"Sounds like a good idea to me." Cody's mouth came down on hers once again.

Andy might be getting impatient, but he would be going with Dorinda when the circus left Abilene; Cody would not.

237

As Michael Hirsch passed between two wagons carrying a bucket of water, he saw Andy. Michael hesitated, then set the bucket down and hurried over to say hello to his new friend.

"Hi, Andy," Michael said, noticing that Andy seemed bothered about something. "What's wrong?"

Andy glanced around. "Oh, hello, Michael. You want to know what's wrong?" He jerked a thumb at the couple embracing nearby. "That's what's wrong. Somebody not keeping her mind on business."

Michael took a closer look at the man and woman and suddenly realized who they were. "Hey, that's Cody!" he exclaimed.

"That's right. And it looks like Dorinda's gone all moony over him." Andy slowly shook his head. "That's not good. Not when you work with guns. You've got to concentrate on what you're doing."

Michael started to point out that the same statement could apply to Cody but then stopped. He was bothered as he watched Cody kiss Dorinda Russell. When it came to romance, he was pretty well lost.

Ever since they had come to Abilene, Michael had figured that sooner or later his sister, Agnes, and Cody Fisher would end up together. He knew that Agnes liked Cody, and Michael worshiped him. So it would have been perfectly all right with him if Cody and Agnes had decided to get married. But he could see with his own eyes just how interested Cody was in Dorinda.

Michael shook his head. There was nothing he could do about Cody and Dorinda—or Cody and Agnes, for that matter. Grownups usually did what they wanted. They could work out their own problems, because they certainly did not listen to advice from kids.

"I see you've still got the job," Andy said, breaking into Michael's train of thought.

"What?" Michael asked.

"The job." Andy pointed at the bucket of water that Michael had been carrying. "You know, hauling water for the animals."

"Oh, yeah. I love it. Some of the other fellows from the orphanage are working with me."

Andy grinned. "From the way you talked about how you were going to get in trouble when you went home last night, I didn't know if we'd see you today or not."

Michael winced at the reminder of the

dressing down he had gotten from Sister Laurel. "I did get in some trouble," he admitted. "But when I told Sister Laurel about how much fun the job was and how I was earning extra money, she decided it wouldn't hurt anything. Might even be a learning experience, she said, and she told the other fellows they could come out here after school and see about hiring on, too."

Andy slapped Michael on the shoulder. "Well, I'm glad you came back. You'll learn a few things if you hang around a circus for long enough. Of course, not all of them are things that a nun would approve of."

That was true enough, Michael thought, glancing again at Cody and Dorinda.

Red Mike's was little more than a shack on Buckeye Street on the northern edge of town. It offered anonymity, whiskey that would burn a hole in your gullet, and one soiled dove whose better days had been about twenty years earlier. The air inside was dimly lit by a couple of lanterns and was full of cigarette smoke. The bar consisted of rough-cut wide planks laid atop whiskey barrels. There were a few rickety tables with uneven legs.

Ned Cahoon was alone when he slouched

into Red Mike's that evening. There was a huge, mottled bruise on his jaw where Cody's final punch had caught him. His whole body ached, and inside him the desire for revenge burned like an inferno. He wondered what the hell he was doing here.

The message had found him late that afternoon, while he and his companions were trying to drink away their aches and pains in another of Abilene's many saloons. A dirty-faced street kid had darted into the place and tugged at his sleeve, thrusting a folded piece of paper into his hand. The kid ran away before Cahoon could ask him what the devil he was doing.

Cahoon had unfolded the paper carefully, and he was glad he did. That way he was able to conceal the bank note he found there. Along with the money was a note promising more if he would come to Red Mike's tonight at nine o'clock.

His first thought was that it was a trap. He had plenty of enemies, and most of them would not hesitate to trick him. It was even possible that Cody Fisher was behind the message.

It was nine now, Cahoon thought as he approached the bar. Whatever was going to happen would happen soon.

"Gimme a whiskey," Cahoon rasped to the bartender. He leaned his left hand on the bar, keeping his right close to the butt of the pistol on that side. His eyes surveyed the room in the dirty mirror behind the bar. There were perhaps a dozen men in the saloon, all of them nursing drinks and minding their own business. The prostitute, her hair dyed an impossible shade of orange, was trying to strike a bargain with one of the customers. Cahoon thought a few of the men looked familiar, but he could not place any of them.

He sipped the fiery liquor in the glass the bartender shoved toward him and he winced as it burned his scraped mouth. The squeal of the batwing hinges made him glance over his shoulder.

A dark-haired man in a suit came into the dingy little saloon. With a pronounced limp he walked toward the bar.

Cahoon stiffened and quickly put his drink back on the bar. He recognized the newcomer as the man who had put up the circus handbills—the man Cahoon and his friends had tried to rough up a few days earlier. For a moment, it occurred to Cahoon that the cripple had set up this meeting as a trap to get back at him for having picked a fight. Some of the circus roustabouts might be waiting outside to jump him. If that was the case, they would get more than they bargained for.

The man with the limp spotted Cahoon and started toward him. He stepped up to the bar next to Cahoon and hissed, "Take it easy. You look like you're about ready to go for your gun."

Cahoon did not relax. "What the hell are you doing here?"

"I sent for you," Gil Palmer said. "But don't worry. It's not a trap, if that's what you're thinking. Why don't I buy you a drink?"

Without taking his eyes off Palmer, Cahoon tossed off the rest of his whiskey. "Why don't you do that?"

Palmer signaled for the bartender to refill Cahoon's glass and said, "Bring me a beer." When both men had their drinks, Palmer suggested, "Why don't we go sit down and talk about why I arranged this meeting?"

Cahoon, still suspicious, nodded and said, "Sure."

They carried their drinks to a vacant table in a corner. Keeping his voice low, Palmer said, "I hear you've had some trouble with those circus folk."

Cahoon hunched over his glass of whiskey. "What if I have?" he answered in surly tones. "What business is it of yours? Ain't you one of them?"

Palmer lifted the mug of beer to his lips and sipped from it. "I may work for the circus," he said, "but I'm no longer one of them." He slapped his bad leg. "Not since the day I got this bum leg. I've been working on it, exercising it and strengthening it while no one's around, but it will never be the same. And neither will I."

Cahoon peered across the table at the former acrobat. There was something in the tone of Palmer's voice that Cahoon recognized—the sound of a man seeking vengeance. A sly smile spread across Cahoon's bruised face. "Reckon you've got a score to settle with that there circus, then."

Palmer nodded slowly. "Yes. Yes, I do, and you can help me, Mr. Cahoon."

"Why the hell would I want to do that?"

"For two reasons. One, you could do some score-settling yourself, and two, my plan could mean a great deal of money for you."

Cahoon's interest quickened at the mention of money. He leaned back in his chair and finished off his drink. "Tell me what you've got in mind," he said.

Palmer pushed his unfinished beer aside. "At every performance, after all the spectators have been admitted, the ticket receipts are taken into a small tent near the entrance to the big top. The money is counted there and then locked into a metal box. The box is taken to Jeffries's wagon and put in a safe there. It would be very easy to get into that tent while the money is being counted and take it. Everyone's attention will be on the big tent where the show is going on. Usually, there's no one in the small tent except Jeffries's bookkeeper. He won't be any trouble."

Cahoon nodded thoughtfully. "Sounds like it might work," he admitted.

"You could do the job easily with a couple of your friends."

"What would you get out of this?" Cahoon asked.

Palmer smiled. "Satisfaction . . . and a fourth of the loot."

Cahoon pulled the makings from his vest pocket and started to roll a cigarette as he thought over the proposition. He was always willing to make some easy money, and the job Palmer was proposing sounded simple enough.

There was also the chance that if there was any gunplay, some stray bullets might find their way to that fancy pants Dorinda Russell and that hotshot marshal and deputy. He might be able to settle several scores in one night.

"I'll do it," Cahoon said with an abrupt nod.

"Good!" Palmer's eyes were fierce as he said it.

Cahoon scratched a match into life on his thumbnail and lit the cigarette. As he blew out the first lungful of smoke, he commented, "I'm surprised you want to cause trouble for those folks, Palmer. After all, that ringmaster feller gave you a job after you got hurt."

Palmer's eyes glazed over momentarily, as if he was looking deep within himself. He said tonelessly, "I don't care about me. I knew the risks; I knew I was pushing myself. But after my fall, that bastard should have made the rest of them use a net. He let his own wife go up there without any protection—and now she's dead." Palmer's voice broke, and his eyes closed. "And now she'll never know how I felt about her."

Cahoon shifted in his seat, slightly uncomfortable at hearing the revelation.

Palmer opened his eyes again, blinked rapidly for a second, and composed himself. He reached over and picked up his mug of beer. "Shall we drink to success?" he asked.

"Sure, soon as I get some more whiskey over here." Cahoon caught the bartender's eye and jerked his head to bring over a bottle.

Shot glass and beer mug clinked together a moment later. "To the ultimate fate of Professor Jericho Jeffries's Traveling Circus and Extravaganza," Gil Palmer whispered.

Cahoon recognized the expression on the man's face as he drank. It was the look of a man who lived for revenge. He had seen it a few times himself . . . in a mirror.

XII

As promised, Travis and Cody were on hand that night for the circus's performance. Both lawmen remained alert during the show, but nothing went wrong. The crowd was almost as big as the one for the opening performance, and as Jeffries had stated, most of the acts had new tricks to try out, along

with new wrinkles on the old ones. Everyone in attendance seemed to have a good
time.

After the performance Cody was on hand
at Dorinda Russell's wagon when the trick
shooter returned to the vehicle. She smiled
when she saw him waiting.

"What did you think of that new trick?"
she asked immediately.

Cody grinned. "If I was Andy, I couldn't
just stand there and let you shoot a cigarette
out of my mouth. I'm not that brave."

"You're brave enough," Dorinda said.
"Help me put this stuff away."

She was holding several targets, and Cody
took them from her and carried them into
the wagon. He was acutely aware that the
two of them were alone, but he was surprised by the eagerness with which Dorinda
came into his arms once he had put the
targets down.

He kissed her for a long moment, then
said, "I wasn't sure what would happen
when I came to see you tonight."

"I was sure," Dorinda whispered.

Cody's hands strayed down to the gun
belt around Dorinda's waist. Carefully he
undid the buckle and lifted the belt and
holsters free. Reaching behind him with one

hand, he placed them on the floor. That was a switch, he thought wryly as his lips found hers again. Usually it was the woman taking his gun belt off. . . .

"You look pleased with yourself this morning," Travis said as Cody strolled into the office the next day.

"I'm just pleased with the whole world," Cody said. He went to the stove and poured himself a cup of coffee.

"Didn't see you around after the circus's performance last night," the marshal observed.

"Oh, I was around. I was keeping an eye on some of the performers."

Travis did not say anything for a moment, and that gave Cody the uneasy feeling that the marshal knew exactly what he had been doing. But he was not going to explain or apologize. He felt a genuine affection for Dorinda Russell, not to mention his admiration for her sharpshooting skills.

Finally Travis said, "I talked to Jeffries after the show. He said they're going to put on two more performances, then pull out the day after tomorrow. That'll give them time to repair their wagons and get some of the horses reshod, the ones that need it. I'll be glad to see them go."

"Yeah," Cody said, his voice sounding slightly hollow. "They have brought a lot of trouble to town."

"Seen Cahoon around since that brawl yesterday?"

Cody touched his bruised face. The pain was less severe today, although the bruise was turning an ugly shade of yellow. "He's probably holed up somewhere. Maybe he's had enough."

Travis shook his head. "Not Cahoon. You're underestimating him, Cody. Whenever he makes a move again, I hope it's still here in Abilene. I don't want him following the circus when they leave. There's some lonely country out there, some places where they couldn't get any help at all."

Cody frowned. He had not considered that possibility. "Maybe we ought to throw Cahoon in jail for a while."

"On what charge?"

"How about disturbing the peace? That ruckus yesterday ought to qualify."

"I'll think about it." Travis nodded.

Behind Cody the door opened, and he glanced over his shoulder as Thurman Simpson came into the office. The schoolteacher was wearing his usual dark suit and string tie, but his face was red with anger.

"Marshal, you've got to do something!" he declared.

Travis picked up his cup of coffee from the desk and sipped. "Shouldn't you be in school at this time of day, Mr. Simpson?" he said.

"I was," Simpson snapped. "I endured the taunts of the town ruffians and layabouts on my way to the schoolhouse, but I simply cannot teach a class with them congregating just outside, laughing and carousing!"

Travis pushed his chair back and stood up. "What's this all about?"

"It's . . . it's that damned horse!" Simpson sputtered. "They're calling me a pony-killer!"

Cody almost choked on his coffee as he laughed. "Word of that got out, did it?"

Simpson spun toward him. "I don't doubt that you spread the story," he accused. "That's the kind of venomous thing you'd do, Deputy."

"Now just hold on," Travis said. "Cody, did you tell anybody about what happened here?"

Cody shook his head. "Nope. But I'm not surprised folks found out about it. It's hard to keep it a secret when you've got a hardened criminal like Mr. Simpson here in your midst."

Travis gave his deputy a warning look and then said to Simpson, "I'll make sure folks understand that you weren't arrested."

Simpson pulled a handkerchief from his breast pocket and mopped his face. "See that you do. It's gotten so bad that some of my students are referring to me as a jail-bird!"

Cody laughed again in spite of his resolve not to. It was good to see a pompous ass like Simpson taken down a notch or two.

Simpson glared murderously at him for a moment, then spun on his heel and stalked out of the office.

Still chuckling, Cody asked Travis, "Did he ever bring you that hundred dollars for the horse?"

Travis nodded. "I gave it to Jeffries. And I was hoping that would be the end of it. *Did* you tell anybody about it, Cody?"

"I swear I didn't, Marshal. But the way it sounds to me, Simpson's getting what he deserves."

"Well, no matter how it sounds to you, I want you to go down to the school and get rid of those fellows who are bothering him.

Tell them to go back to the saloons, or I'll throw them in jail for unlawful assembly."

Cody reached for his hat. "Sure thing, Marshal." He was still grinning as he left the office.

When he reached the schoolhouse, he found a half dozen of the loafers who usually hung out in the Alamo Saloon. They were passing a bottle back and forth and telling lewd stories, most of which had Thurman Simpson in leading roles. Their voices were loud enough to carry clearly into the school.

"Howdy, boys," Cody said to them.

"Mornin', Deputy," one of the men replied. He had the bottle in his hand at the moment, and he extended it toward Cody. "You need a little of this?"

Cody shook his head. "No, thanks. The marshal sent me down here to tell you boys to move along. Seems you're disrupting the youngsters' schooling in there."

"Hell, we was just havin' some fun," another man said. "That there schoolteacher thinks he's so high and mighty—"

"I know, I know," Cody said, nodding. "But I reckon it'd be best if you move along anyway."

Grumbling, the men started back toward

Texas Street. Cody had a feeling they might be back, but at least he had done his job and followed Travis's orders.

Cody had made a date for that afternoon with Dorinda, and shortly after noon, he went to the livery stable and rented a buggy. When he drove up to the circus camp and found Dorinda waiting at her wagon, she smiled up at him in surprise. Cody lifted a wicker basket from the floorboard of the buggy. The basket was covered with a clean white cloth, and several delicious aromas drifted from it.

"How long's it been since you went on a picnic?" He grinned.

Dorinda clapped her hands in delight. "What a wonderful idea! Let me get my bonnet."

Cody watched her with admiration as she went into the wagon. She was wearing a simple cotton dress today, light blue with white ruffles at the wrists and bosom. For the first time since Cody had known her, she looked like a simple farm girl rather than an experienced circus trouper. He liked this look as much as he had all of her others.

Dorinda came back with a blue bonnet fastened over her long hair. Cody hopped down from the seat of the buggy and helped her up.

They drove away from the camp, heading west. Cody, familiar with the territory, knew that a mile or so away was a small creek that wound between wooded, rolling hills. The first wildflowers of the spring were starting to bloom, and Dorinda exclaimed at their beauty.

Cody easily found the creek, picked a shady spot under a tree, and spread the blanket he had brought along. They sat down to delve into the basket of food Cody had ordered from the café—fried chicken, mashed potatoes, peas, biscuits, and a tin of deep-dish apple pie.

Leaning against the tree trunk, Cody slowly ate one of the drumsticks. A fresh breeze riffled the flowers and the tall grass, and the sound of the creek bubbling close by was plainly audible. Cody felt a sense of peace and contentment stealing over him.

He lifted one of the bottles of beer that had been in the basket, tilted it to his lips, and swallowed thirstily. Then he drew a deep breath and in a hoarse whisper said, "I wish you didn't have to go, Dorinda."

She did not look up to meet his intent gaze. "There's a part of me that wishes the same thing, Cody," she said softly. "But the circus is my life. It has been for a long time now. I was really still a child when I left home to go with Professor Jeffries. I don't know anything else."

Cody grimaced and looked off in the distance, studying the fluffy white clouds that wafted through the deep-blue Kansas sky. "How'd you wind up being a trick-shot artist, anyway?"

Dorinda smiled as she answered. "I had a father and five older brothers, and all of them were hunters. I knew how to fire a gun almost before I could walk. It's just a natural talent, I suppose."

"But you've worked hard at it."

"Damn right I have. I know a lady's not supposed to talk that way, but it's the way I feel. I'm proud of what I've done. I've entertained a lot of people, and because of that I've been able to help my folks back in Illinois pay the bills." Now her eyes looked into his as she went on. "You don't seem to mind that I'm good with a gun."

Cody shook his head. "No reason I should. We all try to do what we're best at. Guns or not, you're about the best-looking woman I've ever seen—and the nicest."

Her face flushed with pleasure at the compliment. "Thank you. I think you're special, too."

Cody looked at the picnic basket and swallowed. "You think this food will keep a while longer?"

Dorinda smiled again. "I think it will," she said as Cody moved closer and took her in his arms.

Music came from the big top, the happy sound of the circus band's accompaniment for one of the clown acts. Professor Jericho Jeffries's Traveling Circus and Extravaganza had been under way for almost a quarter of an hour. At the ticket booth the steady stream of customers had dried up as soon as the performance had begun.

The door at the rear of the small ticket booth opened, and a white-haired man carrying a canvas bag came out of the little building. He headed for a tent several yards away.

From the shadows between two wagons, three figures watched the white-haired man. Ned Cahoon, Mitch Stark, and Hack Dawson all wore long dusters and had bandannas over their faces. Cahoon nudged Mitch and whispered, "That must be the bookkeeper."

"Yeah," Mitch replied. "And that must be the money. Let's go get it!"

"Hold on," Dawson cautioned. "Wait until he's in the tent, like Ned planned."

"That's right," Cahoon said. He had decided to let Stark and Dawson think that he had planned this job. They did not have to know about Palmer's part in it until it was time to split the money. They would not kick too much about giving up a fourth of the loot; they were too much under Cahoon's thumb to complain for long.

The bookkeeper pushed through the tent's entrance, and a moment later there was a flare of light inside the tent as the man lit a lantern.

Cahoon slipped his right-hand Colt from its holster. "Let's go," he said.

The sideshows were on the other side of the big top, so they did not have to worry about being spotted from there. The area on this side of the tent was used primarily for work and storage. Many of the plain wagons, as opposed to the brightly painted ones in which the performers traveled, were parked over here. The trio, led by Cahoon, catfooted its way through the shadows and approached the bookkeeping tent.

"All right," Cahoon hissed as they paused

just outside the entrance. "The old man won't give us any trouble. Let's just get in and out as quick as we can."

The other two nodded their understanding.

Cahoon's left arm swept aside the canvas flap over the entrance, and brandishing the gun, he burst into the tent, Stark and Dawson on his heels. The white-haired man was sitting at a table with folding money and coins spread out in front of him. His head jerked up, and he stared in shock at the armed, masked apparitions confronting him.

"Don't move, old man!" Cahoon barked. "Keep those hands in sight!"

The bookkeeper kept his hands on the tabletop. He quavered, "What . . . what is this?"

"What the hell does it look like?" Cahoon demanded. "It's a robbery, you old fool! Now get that money gathered up and put it in that box." Cahoon gestured with his gun barrel toward the open metal box on the table.

Slowly the bookkeeper shook his head. A stubborn look crept onto his face. "You can't do this," he declared. "You can't get away with it."

"The hell we can't!" Mitch Stark blustered, stepping forward and waving his gun in the old man's face. "Do what we tell you, or I'll put a bullet in you, you old bastard!"

The bookkeeper's face turned crimson with rage. "You little thief!" he snapped. "I'll teach all three of you a lesson—"

He lunged up from his chair, moving with surprising speed, and reached out to grab Stark's gun.

"Look out!" Dawson cried.

"Goddammit!" Cahoon yelled. The whole plan was falling apart right in front of his eyes. But he was not going to allow that to happen. He grabbed Stark's shoulder and shoved him aside, opening a clear path to the bookkeeper.

Cahoon lashed out with the revolver in his hand. The barrel thudded against the bookkeeper's head, staggering him. Rage gripped Cahoon, and he swung twice more, slashing the weapon across the old man's face, ripping his flesh and knocking teeth from his mouth. With a moan the bookkeeper put his hands to his bloody features and fell forward across the table, rolling off to sprawl motionlessly on the ground.

"Damn, Ned," Hack Dawson breathed, "you killed him!"

Cahoon grated, "Who cares? Grab that money, you idiots!"

Dawson and Stark went to their knees and began rapidly gathering the money that the bookkeeper's collapse had scattered. In a matter of moments, they had the night's receipts stuffed into the small metal box. Cahoon jerked his head toward the tent's entrance and said, "Come on!"

He had taken one step toward the flap, his gun still in his hand, when it was shoved aside, and a tall, bald man in a leopard-skin costume blocked the opening.

Bruno Wagner's mouth dropped open in surprise as he confronted Cahoon and the others. His eyes darted around the interior of the tent, taking in the scene. A growl rose in his throat as he spotted the book-keeper's body.

Letting out a howl, Bruno lunged forward, one arm whipping around and backhanding Mitch Stark across the face. Stark's chin seemed to slide out of place as his jaw was smashed by the blow. He was thrown back against the side of the tent.

Dawson's hands still held the metal box containing the loot. That left it up to Cahoon. Faced with the raging strong man,

Cahoon took the only course he saw open. He jerked his Colt up and triggered a shot.

The bullet caught Bruno in the left shoulder, punching through muscle and knocking him backward. Bruno grunted in pain as he fell half in and half out of the tent. Clutching his shoulder with his right hand, he tried to get back to his feet, but the effort and shock of being shot were too much for him. With a groan he fell back, out cold.

Cahoon spun to face the stunned Dawson. Hack was standing with his mouth open, while Stark writhed and whimpered in pain on the ground nearby. "Dammit, come on," Cahoon rasped, jamming his gun back in its holster. "Grab Mitch, and let's get the hell out of here!"

"That shot's gonna bring folks runnin'!" Dawson said frantically.

"I know!" Cahoon bent and grasped Stark's arm, hauling him to his feet. Putting his face close to Stark's, Cahoon asked urgently, "Can you run, Mitch?"

There was no way Cahoon could leave him behind to talk and identify them. If Stark could not get away, he would have to die here.

As Stark nodded shakily, Cahoon rasped,

"Then come on." He would at least give Stark a chance.

With Cahoon in the lead, the three men plunged out of the tent toward the grove of trees where their mounts were hidden, about twenty yards from the edge of the camp. Cahoon paused long enough to rip the money box from Dawson's hands. "I'll take care of that," he snarled.

"Hey, wait a minute—"

"You want to stand around here arguin' and get shot for your trouble?" Cahoon demanded.

Dawson shook his head. He reached out to support Stark instead as the smaller man started to sag.

"Let's go," Cahoon said. He started to run through the shadows, not looking back to see if the other two were following him.

Travis and Cody were admiring the skill with which Count Lothar von Benz was putting his big cats through their paces when they heard the gunshot. The two lawmen exchanged a quick glance, and then they were both running toward the big top's entryway.

Cody reached it first, with Travis a step behind. The deputy plunged out past the canvas flap, his gun drawn. His eyes darted around the surrounding camp, looking for the source of trouble.

Some of the spectators had heard the disturbance, too, and curious shouts were coming from the tent. The count stopped his act and glared toward the entryway where Travis and Cody had gone rushing out.

A low moan drew Cody's attention. Spotting Bruno lying in the entrance of a small tent, Cody said, "Over there, Marshal!" He ran toward the bloody form of the strong man.

Travis hung back slightly, his head swiveling as he watched for any threat. Cody charged recklessly ahead, as was his nature, knowing that Travis would be ready if anybody tried to ambush them.

Cody dropped to one knee beside Bruno. The strong man's shoulder and arm were covered with blood, and Cody could see the bullet hole in the flesh. Bruno shook his head and tried to open his eyes. Cody leaned closer and said urgently, "What happened, Bruno? Who did this to you?"

Bruno lifted his uninjured arm slightly and pointed into the tent. "In . . . th-there . . ." he gasped.

Travis was standing beside Cody now and

heard the big man's answer. He put a hand on Cody's shoulder and said, "I'll check it out." Colt up and ready, he moved past Bruno into the tent.

Travis saw immediately that the tent held no threat. He saw the pistol-whipped body of the bookkeeper, recognizing him from the night before, when Jeffries had introduced him to the man. There were also a few coins scattered on the ground inside the tent, Travis saw as he knelt to check on the old man's condition. He was alive, Travis discovered, but breathing shallowly and raggedly.

Travis came to his feet and hurried outside, where a crowd was gathering around Bruno's body. Jeffries was among the group, and Travis grabbed his arm. "Send someone for Dr. Bloom," the marshal ordered sharply. "Your bookkeeper's inside the tent. He's been pistol-whipped, from the looks of it, but he's still alive."

"Who—who would do such a dreadful thing?" Jeffries demanded.

"Whoever stole your receipts for tonight," Travis said. "Come on, Cody. They can't have gotten far."

Leaving Jeffries and the others to care for Bruno and the bookkeeper until Aileen

Bloom could arrive, Travis and Cody slipped into the shadows cast by the cluster of circus wagons.

In a whisper, Cody asked, "You think whoever did it is still around here, Marshal?"

"Did you hear any horses leaving after that shot?"

"Nope."

"Neither did I," Travis said. "And I haven't heard any hoofbeats since then. We were out of the big tent within a minute or two of the robbery, Cody. We would have heard the thieves making a getaway."

Cody grinned in the shadows. "Then they're still in the camp somewhere, probably trying to get to wherever they stashed their horses."

"That's the way I figure it."

"And I'd bet my saddle it was Ned Cahoon who pulled this."

"No bet," Travis said grimly.

They had been moving quietly but quickly between the wagons as they talked. Now they fell silent, concentrating on the task at hand. When they reached the edge of the camp, Travis motioned for Cody to go one direction while he headed the other way. Cody nodded in understanding.

Moonlight illuminated the open areas and

created deep shadows in other places. Cody and Travis were about fifty yards apart when a figure suddenly loomed up in front of Travis. The marshal tilted his Colt in that direction and was only an instant from pressing the trigger when he recognized one of the roustabouts from the circus.

"Don't shoot, Marshal!" the man squawked, holding his hands aloft. One of them held a whiskey bottle. "I was just out here havin' a drink. No call to get upset."

Travis bit back a curse and said, "You see anybody out here the last couple of minutes?"

The man shook his head and then pointed toward the rebuilt corral where the large animals were kept. "No, I ain't seen nobody, but I did hear somethin' funny over there just now. Sounded almost like somebody cryin'—"

Travis's eyes flicked toward the corral, and he spotted moonlight glinting on metal. "Get down!" he shouted at the roustabout, lunging forward and giving the man a hard shove.

The roustabout went sprawling as a gunshot cracked from the corral. The slug whapped through the air close to Travis's head. He snapped the Colt up, triggered twice, saw movement in the shadows, and fired again. A man came staggering into the moonlight, his hands pressed to his middle. He took two steps before he pitched forward onto this face.

Running footsteps came from Travis's right, and he lunged forward, catching himself on one hand as another gun blasted and sent a bullet over his head. He fired quickly at the sprinting figure, knowing he probably would not hit him. "Cody!" he shouted. "Coming your way!"

Travis had no way of knowing how many men he was up against. He had seen two so far, but there might be others. He hurried forward to crouch behind a wagon wheel. His gun was lined on the man he had shot, but there was no motion from the dark shape on the ground. Travis knew from grim experience that the man was probably dead, but he was not going to bet his life on that. He made his way forward carefully, using what cover he could find.

Cody had spun around at the sound of shots and he was already moving toward Travis when he heard the marshal's warning yell. Cody spotted the man running toward him and cried out, "Hold it, mister!"

The man's reply was a shot, the slug

whining through the night. Cody returned the fire and saw the man swerve away from him. The man ran desperately toward the big top, cut off from any other avenue of escape.

Cody pounded after him. The deputy feared that if the thief made it to the crowd around the big top, he would grab one of the bystanders and use him or her as a shield. Cody did not want that to happen.

He was too late, he thought bitterly as he heard a scream up ahead. Rounding a wagon at top speed, he jerked to a halt as he saw a horrifying tableau in front of him.

A thick-set man wearing a duster had grabbed a little girl who had been attending the performance with her family. Now, as the crowd scattered around him, he pressed the barrel of his pistol to the girl's head.

"Get away!" he screeched. "All of you, get away from me, or I'll kill her! I swear I'll kill her!"

Cody's mouth was dry and his throat felt constricted. The bandanna once tied around the outlaw's face had slipped down so that his features were revealed, and Cody recognized him as Hack Dawson, one of Cahoon's friends. Dawson's face glistened with sweat, his eyes darting in nervous panic as he scanned the crowd in front of him. He was clearly scared enough to carry out his threat.

As the man's darting eyes lit on Cody, the deputy said, "Take it easy, Dawson. Nobody wants to hurt you." He tried to keep his voice calm and level, but it was not easy.

"Back off, Deputy!" Dawson warned.

Cody held up both hands, the Colt still in his right one. "I'm backing off," he said as he took a step backward. "It'll be all right, mister. Just let the little girl go."

The girl was writhing in terror. Hoarse whimpers came from her throat. Cody did not recognize her. In her feed-sack dress and pigtails, she looked like any of several dozen farm kids from the area. He wondered fleetingly which of the fear-stricken onlookers were her parents.

Suddenly, a man pushed his way through the crowd and stepped out into the little clearing that had formed around the outlaw and his hostage. Count Lothar von Benz strode forward. "Release that child!" he said firmly.

The hardcase turned slightly. "Get out of here, mister!"

"I said let her go!" the count barked.

Crazy Prussian son of a bitch, Cody wanted

270

to shout at the count. He was going to get them all killed.

The outlaw jerked his gun toward von Benz, and the girl sagged in the grip of his other arm, slipping toward the ground.

That was the opening Cody needed. He yanked the Colt down and squeezed the trigger, the motion so fast it was a blur. The bullet smacked into the gunman's head, knocking him off his feet and right out from under his hat, which fell onto his face, obscuring the bloody ruin. As he fell dead onto his back, his gun slipped unfired from his still-twitching fingers. Free now, the little girl ran toward her parents, bawling at the top of her lungs.

Cody looked from the body to the count. Von Benz smiled thinly. "You must never let the beasts forget who is in command," he said.

Cody took a deep breath and found himself grinning with relief.

Travis appeared behind Cody. "There's another one back there at the edge of the camp," the marshal said as he looked bleakly at the gunman's body. "He's as dead as that one. Both of them rode with Cahoon."

Cody nodded. "You see any sign of Cahoon himself?"

"No. And that means he may still be around. I don't think these two would pull a job like this alone."

Cody's eyes met Travis's. As long as Ned Cahoon was out there somewhere in the night, no one was safe.

Cahoon crouched, leaning against one of the wagons. He clutched the money box in one hand; the other held his pistol. He lifted his right arm and used the sleeve of the duster to wipe sweat off his forehead. His hand was trembling slightly. He frowned at it.

Dawson and Stark were both dead, more than likely, to judge from the amount of shooting that had gone on after they split up. He did not think either one of them had noticed when he slipped away. All he had to do now was get out of this camp somehow and make it to the horses. If he could do that, they would never catch him. Ned Cahoon would head for the high lonesome country, and to hell with everybody else, including Gil Palmer!

Cahoon swallowed nervously. This was the first time he had been facing odds like this, and he did not like it. He had to get moving again, had to get out of here.

He hurried around the end of the wagon,

then stopped in his tracks and jerked back as he almost ran into someone. "Goddamn!" he yelped, lifting the gun in his hand.

"Hold it, Cahoon!" the shadowy figure hissed. "It's me, you fool!"

"Palmer!" Cahoon breathed the name in relief. A moment earlier, he had decided to double-cross the former acrobat, but all of those thoughts deserted him as he said desperately, "Listen, Palmer, you've got to help me get out of here!"

Palmer nodded. "Sure, Cahoon," he said. His hand slipped inside his coat, and when it came out, he was holding a small pistol. He jabbed it toward Cahoon's chest and squeezed the trigger.

The bullet felt like a fist thumping Cahoon in the chest. He felt a sudden fire inside him, and he dimly realized that Palmer had just shot him. Cahoon tried to lift the gun in his hand, but it was just too heavy.

Palmer fired again. Cahoon rocked back, falling to the ground, dropping his gun and the money box. One booted foot drummed on the dirt for a second, and then the outlaw was completely still.

Palmer took a deep breath. The wheels of his brain were spinning, just as they had been ever since he had realized that the robbery had gone badly. When he had set out looking for Cahoon among the wagons, he had not been sure what he would do if he found him. When the time came, however, it had all been so simple. Palmer knew he would not have been able to sneak Cahoon out of the camp. And if he left Cahoon alive, the man could be captured and reveal Palmer's part in the scheme. That had left only one course open.

Palmer had only seconds in which to act. He bent over and scooped up the money box, then ran to an empty animal cage nearby. It was unlocked, and a thick layer of straw covered the floor. Yanking the door open, Palmer hopped lithely into the cage. He shoved the metal box deep into the straw, then dropped back onto the ground and hurried over to Cahoon's body.

People were approaching now, several of them bearing torches. In the lead were Luke Travis and Cody Fisher, both of them with their guns out and ready.

"It's all right," Palmer called, turning toward them and taking a couple of steps in his exaggerated limp. "Cahoon's over there. He's dead."

"What happened?" Travis asked as Cody went to check the body.

Palmer still had the little gun in his hand. He lifted it and shook his head. "I—I'm not sure," he said slowly. "He nearly ran over me while he was trying to get away . . . and then he raised his gun and was going to shoot me. I didn't have a choice, Marshal. I shot first."

"Mighty damned lucky," Travis commented.

Palmer passed a shaking hand over his face. "I know."

Cody stood up from his crouch beside Cahoon's body and came over to them. "He's dead, all right," the deputy confirmed. "That was good shooting, Palmer."

"Like the marshal said, I was lucky."

Professor Jericho Jeffries came up to Palmer and reached out to grasp his hand. Wringing it heartily, he said, "Thank God you were here, Gil! You've disposed of a notorious criminal. Perhaps now the rest of our stay in Abilene won't be quite so hazardous. You have the appreciation of all of us!"

Palmer put a weak smile on his face. "You're welcome, Professor. I wish it hadn't come down to shooting, though."

"It always does with Cahoon's kind," Travis said heavily. He sighed. "Well, I guess I'd better see about taking care of the bodies."

"Excuse me, Marshal, but have you located the missing money?" Jeffries asked.

"Neither of the other two had it," Travis said. "What about Cahoon, Cody?"

The deputy shook his head. "I didn't see any loot, Marshal."

"It would have been in a small metal box," Jeffries said.

Under Travis's direction, a quick search of Cahoon's body and the surrounding area was carried out. The money was not found.

"Cahoon either dropped it while he was trying to get away or stashed it somewhere," Travis speculated. "We'll be able to do a thorough search in the morning. I'm sure it'll turn up, Professor."

"I hope so," Jeffries fretted. "A night's receipts are important to this circus, Marshal."

Palmer tried not to smile as he heard the ringmaster's worried tones. The money in itself was not that important to the former aerialist, but its loss was one more step in his plan to ruin Jeffries. One more step on the road to revenge for Mary's death . . . and the money would come in handy when he eventually took over the circus, Palmer thought.

He let himself be led away by other members of the troupe, all of them congratulating him on his daring confrontation with Cahoon. Travis told Cody to keep an eye on the bodies, then faced the curious spectators who had poured out of the big tent.

"Might as well get back to your seats, folks," Travis told them. "All the excitement's over for tonight out here."

XIII

The excitement may have been over for the night, but the work went on. Dr. Aileen Bloom, who was in the circus audience, tended to both Bruno Wagner and the pistol-whipped bookkeeper. The old man had a possible skull fracture, a certain concussion, and several large cuts on his face. His condition was grave, but Aileen expected him to pull through. However, when the circus left Abilene, he would have to remain behind for at least a few weeks of recovery. Bruno's wound was serious but not life-threatening; the bullet had passed through cleanly, missing all the bones in the strong man's shoulder. Aileen cleaned and bandaged the injury, then told him to take it easy for a couple of weeks. "No more bending iron bars for a while," she warned him. "You've got to give that wound time to heal."

"All right," Bruno promised reluctantly. "I don't know what the show will do without me, though."

Jeffries was standing close by as Aileen ministered to Bruno. He said dryly, "I expect we'll muddle through some way, old chap."

Travis took Ned Cahoon's guns and other belongings and turned the body over to Abilene's undertaker, who was also the local coroner. The man loaded Cahoon's corpse into his wagon, which was already burdened with the remains of Mitch Stark and Hack Dawson. "We'll hold an inquest tomorrow," the undertaker told Travis. "Just a formality, though."

Travis nodded and then drew Cody aside. He said quietly, "I'm going to stay out here tonight, just to make sure nothing else happens. You go back to town, and you can spell me on this duty tomorrow."

Cody frowned. "But Cahoon and his boys

are dead. Who else is going to pull anything?"

"Have you forgotten that a member of the troupe might be sabotaging the circus?" Travis asked.

"Well, yeah, we talked about that, but I figure Cahoon was behind everything that happened since they got here. The rest could be mostly coincidence."

"We'll see," Travis said.

As it turned out, the rest of the night passed quietly. After Jeffries announced that the remainder of that night's performance would be suspended and that everyone holding tickets would be welcome to come back to the final show free of charge, the townspeople and farmers from the audience drifted back to their homes. The animals were returned to their cages, the greasepaint was washed off, and the camp settled down for a peaceful night.

Early the next morning, Jeffries called a meeting of the entire troupe in the big tent.

Travis watched the gathering from the tent's entrance. Jeffries climbed onto one of the pedestals used by Lothar von Benz in his animal-training act. Raising his arms and his voice to get everyone's attention, the ringmaster announced that tonight would be their final performance in Abilene.

"I know that after everything that has happened," Jeffries said, "many of you will be glad to leave here. I know that Marshal Travis will be pleased to see us go."

Jeffries's eyes met Travis's over the crowd, and the marshal touched the brim of his hat acknowledging the comment.

"Now, I want all of you to give tonight's show everything you've got!" Jeffries went on. "The good citizens of Abilene are certainly not to blame for the misfortunes that have befallen us here. They have been unstinting in their support, their applause, their good will. Tonight, we shall pay them back. What do you say?"

The entire troupe let out a cheer. Jeffries might be a hard taskmaster, Travis reflected, but he definitely commanded the affection and respect of his people.

"I'll want to get an early start in the morning. Be sure that all necessary repairs are made today. We'll strike the big top tonight after the performance, as usual, and prepare everything for our early departure. Any questions?"

There were none, and Jeffries concluded by saying, "I thank all of you for your efforts and your devotion. This is still the best circus in the country, bar none!"

Again, the performers and the roustabouts cheered.

Travis spotted Gil Palmer in the crowd, standing near Dorinda Russell and the little clown Andy. Palmer would probably leave today so that he would have a suitable lead on the circus itself. There were other towns to visit and more posters to put up.

As the meeting concluded, Jeffries hopped down from the platform and came over to Travis. "Good morning, Marshal," he said. "I trust you heard all of that."

Travis nodded. "Yes, I did. And you're not completely right about me being glad to see you go. I like some of you folks, Professor. And you did keep life from being boring for a few days."

Jeffries clapped Travis on the shoulder. "Then we've done our job, eh? Now, Marshal, I believe we should start a search for that missing money."

"That's what I was thinking," Travis agreed.

Drafting several roustabouts to help them, Travis and Jeffries spent the morning combing the area where Cahoon had been killed. There was no sign of the money box. Jeffries became more upset as the search failed to turn it up.

"I can afford to lose a night's receipts," he declared, "but I'm damned if I want to!"

Travis shrugged. "I don't know what else we can do, Professor. If you'll leave your traveling schedule with me, I'll sure send the money on to you if it turns up."

Jeffries sighed. "It appears that's all we can do."

Wearily, Travis ran a hand across his tired eyes. "I'm going to head back to town. My deputy will be out here in a little while to keep an eye on things."

"Do you think we'll have more trouble? After all, Cahoon and his cronies are dead."

"I don't know. I'm not of a mind to take chances, though, not after everything that's happened."

Jeffries smiled. "I daresay your associate, Mr. Fisher, will be keeping an eye on our Miss Russell."

Travis grinned back at him. "He does seem to be sweet on her. He's not going to be happy when the show pulls out and she goes with it."

"As she most certainly will. I know Dorinda, Marshal, and as much as she may care about your deputy, she won't give up her traveling life for him."

"I know," Travis said. "I think Cody does, too."

Dorinda slapped leather, pulling the Colt with blinding speed and triggering four fast shots. The empty tin cans that she had lined up on top of some of the corral posts went flying into the air, perforated by the slugs.

Cody came around the corner of the wagon in time to see the demonstration of the young woman's marksmanship. He clapped his hands. "Not bad," he called. "Not flashy, but not bad."

Dorinda shrugged as she slid the gun back in its holster. "I won't bother asking if you can do as well," she said. "I know you can. Shooting at tin cans on posts is nothing."

She did not seem to want to meet his eyes, and he could tell something was bothering her. He moved closer, put a gentle hand on her shoulder, and asked, "What's wrong?"

"Tonight's the last show," she said, still not looking at him.

Cody reached out and cupped her chin, tilting her head back so that she had no choice but to meet his gaze. "Hell, I know that," he said. "And I know you'll be moving on. You don't have to tell me that."

"Oh, Cody—" She leaned against him, pressing her face to his chest. His arms went around her and held her tightly. Dorinda did not cry, but a shudder went through her. "I—I just don't know what to do."

"That's all right," he told her, breathing in the clean fragrance of her hair. "Most folks don't know what they're doing most of the time. But I know what you're going to do, Dorinda."

She looked up at him again. "What, Cody? Tell me."

"You're going to leave with the circus and keep on doing what you've been doing—bringing happiness to folks in every place you put on a show. I know how important that is to you, Dorinda. I'd never ask you to do . . . anything else."

"Like stay here in Abilene?"

For an instant Cody's face seemed carved in stone. Then he smiled and said, "That's right."

A long moment passed while the two of them gazed into each other's eyes, then Dorinda rested her head on Cody's chest again. "Thank you," she whispered. "Thank you for not making it hard on me, Cody."

"You're welcome," he said, and he meant it. But there was a place inside him that was hurting like the very devil.

If anything, Travis thought as he surveyed the crowd inside the big tent, more people were in attendance tonight than had come to the first show. He saw Sister Laurel and Agnes Hirsch and the other orphans. Aileen Bloom and Orion McCarthy and the Reverend Judah Fisher were all there. Most of the people in the audience had attended at least one of the previous shows, but the citizens of Abilene were well aware they might never have another chance to see a circus.

Excitement was running high as Professor Jericho Jeffries ran into the center of the ring to introduce his performers one last time. Sensing the mood of the crowd, the members of the troupe pulled out all the stops, just as Jeffries had requested in the meeting that morning. They were going to give Abilene something to remember.

The trick-riding Carstairs family, Count Lothar von Benz, Dorinda Russell, the acrobats, the clowns—all did their best to top anything that had gone before.

For two solid hours the huge canvas tent was filled with the sounds of laughter and cheers and applause. When the entire troupe came into the ring for a final bow, the ovation lasted for many long minutes.

And then it was over. Much as the children and most of the adults would have liked for it to continue forever, the final performance was done.

The orphans were chattering excitedly as Sister Laurel and Agnes tried to herd them away from the tent and back to the wagons in which they had come. One of them hung back: Michael Hirsch was determined to get one last look at the sights that had thrilled him so.

He and the other boys had been there that afternoon, first thing after school, to do their jobs hauling water and feed. When they were done, Jeffries had paid them their wages and thanked each one of them personally. Tonight there was no longer need for their services. The animal handlers would take care of whatever needed to be done. But come hell or high water, Michael thought as he waited for his chance, he was going to say his own private goodbyes to the elephants and camels and zebras.

When he saw Sister Laurel and Agnes looking in the other direction at the same time, Michael seized the opportunity. He ducked around a wagon and headed for the part of the camp where the animals were kept.

Crouching beside a wagon wheel, he watched, wide-eyed, as the animal handlers herded the majestic beasts back into their compound by torchlight. The large animals were staked out in the corral, and the big cats were put back in their cages. The apes and the bears were back behind the bars of their wagons.

Their work done here, the roustabouts moved on to other tasks. Michael overheard some of them talking about how the big top would be taken down later. *That might be worth staying to see,* he thought. But as soon as the men were gone and the area around the cages and corral was deserted, he slipped out to say farewell to the animals.

"So long, big fella," he whispered to one of the massive elephants as he leaned on the corral fence. He said goodbye to the rest of them, too, and then moved on to the camels and zebras. His chest was tight with emotion. He would never see creatures like these again, he thought, and he was proud that he had helped care for them, even if it had been for only a little while.

Michael moved from wagon to wagon, talking briefly to the animals inside, most of whom regarded him with indifference. That did not matter; he knew they would remember him.

He came around from behind one wagon just as a man hopped down from the vehicle. The man, limping slightly and carrying something in his hands, took a couple of steps before he stopped in his tracks and stared at Michael.

Michael grimaced. He was probably in trouble now, he thought. He was not supposed to be around this part of the camp. In fact he was supposed to be heading back to the orphanage with the rest of the children. But there had not been time to duck back and avoid being seen.

"Hi," Michael ventured, staring at the tall, dark-haired man. The man had a strange, intense expression on his face, and Michael suddenly recognized him as Gil Palmer, the one who traveled ahead of the circus putting up advertising posters. Cody had pointed Palmer out to him.

Cody had also told him about a metal box full of money that had seemingly disappeared. A box about like the one in Palmer's hand . . .

Michael started to back away, but Palmer took a step toward him, a smile on his face now. "You know who I am, don't you, boy?" he asked. He hefted the box. "And you know what's in this, too."

Michael shook his head, instinctively knowing that this was trouble. "I—I don't know anything, mister. I'm just an orphan kid who came to the circus."

"Don't lie to me, boy. Don't ever lie to me!" Suddenly, without warning, Palmer sprang forward toward Michael.

Michael yelped in fear as he whirled around and ran. Palmer's hand grasped his coat for an instant, but then Michael pulled away. This was not the first time he had been chased by an angry adult. Fear gave him added speed.

But Palmer was right behind him! For a man with a bad leg, he was faster than Michael ever would have expected. As the boy raced through the shadowy camp and darted around wagons, Michael tried to figure out what was happening. Palmer must have had something to do with that robbery the night before—

He had gotten that far in his reasoning when he spotted two figures, standing so close together in the moonlight that they looked almost like one. He recognized the hat that the taller figure wore.

"Cody!" Michael shouted.

Cody and Dorinda had found a nice, secluded spot to say their final farewells. They had already decided that he would not come out to the camp the next morning as the circus pulled out. That would have been too painful for both of them. Tonight, they would say goodbye for the last time.

Cody was doing just that, Dorinda wrapped tightly in his arms, when he heard Michael Hirsch's frightened yell.

Cody spun around in time to see Michael running hellbent-for-leather toward him. He reached out and grabbed the boy, hauling him to a stop. "Hold on there, Michael!" Cody said. "What the devil's wrong?"

Michael drew several deep, ragged breaths, trying to get enough air to speak. Before he could say anything, Gil Palmer came pounding up out of the darkness.

Cody looked up and said, "What the hell

is this, Palmer? Were you chasing this boy?" Too late, he spotted the metal box in the man's left hand.

Palmer's hand lashed out, and the box that he held cracked against Cody's head, knocking the deputy to the ground. Ignoring Michael now, Palmer lunged toward Dorinda and grabbed her arm.

He whirled the startled woman around, wrapping his left arm around her neck and cutting off her air. The box in his hand dug painfully into her shoulder. Palmer reached inside his coat with his other hand and brought out a small pistol. He jammed the muzzle of it against Dorinda's temple as Cody started to shake his head groggily and tried to get to his hands and knees.

"Hold it, Deputy!" Palmer grated. "I'll kill her. I swear to God I'll kill her!" His eyes were shining with desperation and hate, all of the façades stripped away. He started backing up, taking Dorinda with him. She had no choice but to go along. Within seconds, both of them had disappeared into the shadows.

Michael leaped to Cody's side and grabbed his arm. "He's crazy, Cody!" the boy cried. "He just started chasing me—"

Leaning on Michael, Cody got to his feet.

A thin line of blood trickled down the side of his face from the cut opened up by the metal box. He shook his head and then took a deep breath.

"Palmer knew more about that robbery than he let on," Cody said as he slipped his gun from its holster. He checked the loads. "He'll use Dorinda as a hostage to try to get out of here alive. You go find Marshal Travis, Michael. He's still around here somewhere."

Michael nodded. "Are you all right, Cody?"

"Better'n Palmer's going to be," Cody replied grimly. "Scoot now."

When Michael began running toward the big top, Cody started in the direction where Palmer and Dorinda had vanished. There was no telling where Palmer would go, not for certain. Cody thought back over the evening and remembered seeing Palmer's wagon parked on the other side of the main tent. He started circling in that direction, the Colt poised in his hand.

Just as the entrance of the big top came in sight, Cody suddenly spotted movement. It was Palmer, he saw with a surge of anger, recognizing the limping gait. The man still had Dorinda with him, dragging her along.

"Palmer!" Cody shouted.

Palmer whirled, putting Dorinda in front of him like a shield. He pulled the gun away from her head long enough to snap a shot at Cody, making the deputy dive behind a wagon. Palmer hauled Dorinda into a run.

Just beyond the big-top entrance Luke Travis appeared in the torchlight. The marshal thrust Michael Hirsch behind him as he brought up his gun.

"Hold it, Palmer!" Travis barked.

Caught in a cross fire, Palmer did the only thing he could. He ducked through the entrance to the big top, taking Dorinda with him.

"Dammit!" Cody said as he ran toward the main entryway. There were several smaller openings around the tent, and Palmer could slip out through any one of them. He and Travis could not cover them all.

The two lawmen reached the main entrance at the same time, pushing through the canvas and then splitting up in case Palmer was waiting to ambush them. The roustabouts had doused most of the torches after the performance ended. In the dim light of the few still shining Cody saw the man in the center of the ring. Dorinda was not fighting him, but she was not helping either, and bringing her along had slowed Palmer down.

Abruptly the flaps of the other openings were thrust back, and several members of the troupe appeared, led by Professor Jericho Jeffries. "My God!" Jeffries exclaimed as he saw Palmer holding Dorinda hostage. He and the others had come to see what all the commotion was about, and this was the last thing they had expected.

Palmer was surrounded now. The only thing protecting him was the gun he held to Dorinda's head. Grimacing, he looked around wildly for an escape. His eyes fell on something that was familiar to him—the ladder leading up to the trapeze platform, far above the dirt of the ring.

Palmer shoved Dorinda toward the ladder. "Climb!" he ordered.

Her face pale with fright, Dorinda put her hands on the rungs and started awkwardly to ascend the ladder. As some of the circus performers started forward, heedless of Palmer's gun, Travis called across the ring, "Stay back!"

Palmer was right behind Dorinda as she climbed. While the others watched, dumbfounded, Jeffries hurried across to Travis and Cody and asked, "What the deuce is going on?"

Travis said, "Palmer's got the money box, and he took Miss Russell as a hostage when Cody saw the box. Is that about the size of it, Cody?"

The deputy nodded, his bloody face bleak. "He must've been in on that robbery with Cahoon, Professor. Could be he's the one who's been causing you trouble all along."

"But why?" Jeffries asked in dismay. "Why would Gil Palmer do such a thing?"

"That's not important now," Travis said. "What's important is getting Miss Russell down from there." He raised his voice again. "All of you folks keep back! Don't do anything to spook him!"

Everyone was looking up, watching the progress of the pair on the ladder. For a second Cody thought about trying to shoot Palmer down, but the angle was too severe. The shot would be too dangerous. If he missed—or even if he hit Palmer and the bullet went right through him—Dorinda could get in the path of the slug.

The few torches still lit were in the lower portion of the tent, leaving its upper regions cloaked in gloom. But enough light reached there for the stunned spectators to see Palmer and Dorinda climb onto the tiny platform where the acrobats usually began their performance. As they balanced there precariously on the perch, Palmer again grabbed Dorinda and pressed the gun to her head.

There was something eerily familiar about the scene. It reminded Cody of the chilling showdown the night before with Cahoon's partner, Dawson. But tonight there would be no distraction in the form of a Prussian animal trainer. Not sixty feet above the ground—and with no net below; it had been taken down earlier, right after the performance.

"Can you hear me, Palmer?" Travis shouted up at them.

"I hear you, Marshal," the answer came back down.

"Why don't you just give up and let that young woman come down? You're not doing yourself any good!"

Palmer shook his head. "The hell I'm not! I'll kill her unless I'm allowed to leave Abilene unharmed with the money."

"I can't let you do that, Palmer! You know that."

"I know I'll kill her, that's what I know! And I'll kill Jeffries, too!"

The ringmaster was unable to contain his

outrage. "Kill me? Why, Palmer? Why would you want to kill me?"

"Because you killed her!" Palmer called down.

Travis, Cody, and Jeffries exchanged anxious, puzzled looks, unsure of what Palmer was talking about.

"You should have made her use a net, you bastard!" Palmer went on. "She's dead because of you, and now she'll never know how much I loved her! All those performances, night after night, working with her . . . and she never knew! Now she never will!"

"Good Lord!" Jeffries breathed, aging years before their eyes. "He's talking about my wife. He's talking about Mary!"

"Palmer's crazy, Marshal," Cody said quietly. "Lord knows how long he's been covering it up."

Travis glanced at Jeffries. "Was there anything between Palmer and your wife?" he asked bluntly.

"If there was, it was only in the man's demented mind," Jeffries responded emphatically. "I'm sure Mary never knew about his feelings."

Travis looked up again. "I understand now, Palmer," he called. "You were getting back at Jeffries when you kept sabotaging his show, weren't you?"

"That's right," Palmer said, looking down past Dorinda's shoulder with a fierce grin. "I was making him pay. I would have taken the circus away from him sooner or later, because it was all that mattered to him. And he took away all that mattered to me—" The man's voice broke.

"If I could just get a shot," Cody muttered.

Travis was frowning as he thought furiously. He called, "That business with the horse being killed and Simpson getting the blame, you did that, didn't you, Palmer?"

Palmer laughed. "It was so damned easy! That schoolteacher prig deserved it, and it was something else to cause trouble for the circus! Just like releasing those animals and getting that fool Cahoon to rob the receipts. I wanted your life to be a living hell, Jeffries, like mine was."

"But I gave you a job after your—" Jeffries began, but Travis cut him off with a hard grip on the arm.

"That's the wrong thing to remind him of," Travis said. "He probably thinks of that as pity on your part, and that's not what he wants."

298

The faint torchlight shone on the tears running down Dorinda's face. In other circumstances she never would have been afraid of a man like Palmer, but this was different. He was insane, and she was in his power. She was shaking so much that the onlookers below could see her trembling.

Travis took a deep breath. "You're not getting out of here, Palmer," he repeated. "You'll be better off if you let Miss Russell go and turn yourself in."

"Never!" Palmer screamed. Suddenly, he jerked the gun away from Dorinda and pointed it down. "I'll take Jeffries to hell with me!"

Cody threw himself at the ringmaster as Palmer's gun cracked. The deputy slammed into Jeffries, knocking him aside, and both men sprawled on the ground as the slug kicked up dust where Jeffries had stood an instant before.

With the gun gone from her head, Dorinda acted. She drove an elbow back into Palmer's middle, staggering him, and tore herself out of his grasp. She stumbled as she pulled away from him, and suddenly her feet slipped off the edge of the little platform. She shrieked as she started to fall, her arms flailing about.

Palmer jerked his gun to the side, trying for another shot at Jeffries. Below, Travis raised his Colt, his arm blurring with the speed of the motion. The heavy pistol blasted against his palm.

At the same instant, Dorinda's fingers slapped the side of the platform, clutching desperately, hanging on to the slight purchase for dear life. Her legs dangled high above the ground.

Palmer staggered again as Travis's bullet caught him in the middle of the body. The metal box, which had been tucked behind his belt during the climb, slipped out, bounced once on the platform, then plummeted to the ground, bursting open when it hit. Money and coins scattered everywhere.

The gun slid from Palmer's fingers as he clutched himself, his hands bloody now. He swayed on the little platform, and then he reached out, reached for something familiar. He clutched the trapeze bar, hooked in position on the railing at one side of the platform. Perhaps the sound of applause and cheers filled his ears as he steadied himself. He might have wanted only to relive past glories.

He launched himself into space, hanging on to the bar, arching high over the stunned onlookers. As he let go of the bar, he kicked into a perfect somersault, then came out of it with hands outstretched toward a catcher who was not there.

His fall seemed to take forever. And there was no net there to catch him.

Cody ignored the bloody form that had been Gil Palmer. He threw himself at the ladder, hauling himself up several rungs at a time. Dorinda was still up there, her grip loosening by the second. He could hear her sobs as he approached, and that spurred him to reckless speed.

He reached the top of the ladder and flung himself across the platform, reaching down to grasp her wrists in a grip of iron. Using his feet to brace himself, he slowly pulled her back up.

When she was on the platform, he grasped her to his chest and held her there, both of them shivering in reaction to what had almost happened. Then, finally, Cody smiled down at her and said softly, "There's one thing you ought to know about me, darling."

"What's that?" Dorinda whispered, her face still wet with tears.

"Well, I kind of forgot about it for a minute, but I am positively terrified of heights."

He started to laugh, and a moment later, she did, too.

XIV

Cody was sitting in a chair in front of the marshal's office, his feet propped on the boardwalk railing, when Travis rode back into Abilene early the next morning.

"They get started down the trail all right?" Cody asked as Travis dismounted and tied his horse at the hitchrack.

"No problems," Travis replied. He stepped up onto the boardwalk. "The professor said to say goodbye to you."

Cody smiled slightly. "They put on a hell of a show, didn't they?"

Travis grunted and went into the office. It had been a strange and bloody week, and he hoped things would stay calm for a while now that the circus had gone.

Cody came into the office a moment later, followed by Sister Laurel. "Good morning, Marshal," the nun said. "Reverend Fisher asked me to stop by and let you know that he's willing to conduct the funeral service for Mr. Palmer, as you requested."

"Good." Travis nodded. He leaned back

in the chair behind the desk. "Palmer may have raised a lot of hell—pardon me, Sister—but I figure he deserves a decent burial. He wasn't all bad."

Cody hung his hat on the hook by the door. "How do you figure that, Marshal, after everything he did?"

Travis met his deputy's questioning gaze. "He also saved that boy's life when the warehouse was on fire. Maybe even saved mine, too, by getting us out through that window. And he risked his own life to do it, without hesitation. No, Palmer had his good points, Cody, and I even liked the man for a while. But something just went wrong in his brain. Something pushed him right to the edge—and then on over."

The door opened as Travis's voice trailed off, and Thurman Simpson marched into the office. Right behind him was a young man in a suit and tie. Travis remembered seeing Simpson's companion around town, but he could not put a name with the face.

Without a greeting Simpson said stiffly, "I hear that you got my hundred dollars back from those circus scoundrels, Marshal."

Travis nodded. "That's right," he said dryly. "It turns out that gun belonged to Gil

Palmer. He put your name on it to throw suspicion on you and create hard feelings between the town and the circus. You've been cleared completely."

Simpson gave one of his rare smiles, and the expression was annoyingly smug. "That's why I brought this reporter along—so that he can tell the whole world that I am an innocent man who was wrongfully accused."

"That's right, Marshal," the young man said as he stepped forward. "I'm Emmett Valentine. I just went to work for the Abilene *Clarion*."

"Glad to meet you, son," Travis said. "I guess you've got your story."

A grin tugged at Cody's mouth as he moved over beside Travis's desk. "Not all the story, Mr. Valentine," he said as he picked up an envelope from the desktop. "Here's the money, Mr. Simpson."

Simpson reached eagerly for the envelope, but Cody kept it just out of his reach.

"I'm glad you brought along this reporter, because now everyone will know just how generous you *really* are."

"I don't know what you mean," Simpson snapped, his hand still outstretched for the money. He eyed Cody suspiciously.

Cody smiled at the reporter. "Mr.

Simpson is just being modest. He told me earlier this morning that he's donating this one hundred dollars to the orphans under Sister Laurel's care so that they can all buy new clothes."

He turned and handed the envelope to the surprised nun as Travis tried hard not to break into laughter. Sister Laurel recovered her composure and said sweetly, "Why, thank you, Mr. Simpson, for your generosity."

Simpson's mouth hung open for a moment. He began to sputter incoherently as Emmett Valentine took out a notepad and began to scribble in it. "This will make a dandy human interest story," the reporter said enthusiastically. "You'll be the talk of the town."

"W-why, y-yes, that's so," Simpson stammered as he realized how he would look if he objected. He swallowed. "Children must have proper clothing, I always say."

"You're so kind, Mr. Simpson," Sister Laurel declared.

Abilene's two lawmen leaned back in their chairs and chuckled with delight.

The publishers hope that this
Large Print Book has brought
you pleasurable reading.
Each title is designed to make
the text as easy to see as possible.
G.K. Hall Large Print Books
are available from your library and
your local bookstore. Or, you can
receive information by mail on
upcoming and current Large Print Books
and order directly from the publishers.
Just send your name and address to:

G.K. Hall & Co.
70 Lincoln Street
Boston, Mass. 02111

or call, toll-free:

1-800-343-2806

A note on the text
Large print edition designed by
Bernadette Montalvo.
Composed in 16 pt Plantin
on a Xyvision 300/Linotron 202N
by Stephen Traiger
of G.K. Hall & Co.